# "You can't keep me here for the night!"

Brance turned around lazily. "But that's what I propose to do."

Mortified, Lindsey blustered, "Nick will have something to say about that!"

"I don't think he will, once he hears that you've spent the night with me."

"You wouldn't . . . !" Lindsey said faintly.

"Wouldn't I?" He crouched to stir up the fire and put the supper pans on to heat. "If I have to stop you marrying someone out of sheer juvenile pique and cussedness, I will."

"It will be your word against mine, of course." Lindsey made an attempt to sound haughty, to cover her very real fear.

"I don't think explanations will come into it," he said easily. "The scandal will be enough to finish you in the eyes of the Mollenda family."

"I can't believe anyone could be so vile!" Lindsey said, glowering. What business was it of his if she married another man to safeguard her father's future?

**Roumelia Lane** has earned a firm place in the world of romance fiction with more than twenty Harlequin Romances to her credit. Originally from England's Brontë country, Yorkshire, the author now lives with her husband on the Mediterranean island of Majorca in a house backed by mountains and overlooking a picturesque village. She has two children and three grandchildren.

## Books by Roumelia Lane

HARLEQUIN ROMANCE

1290—A SUMMER TO LOVE
1338—SEA OF ZANJ
1395—TERMINUS TEHRAN
1478—THE SCENTED HILLS
1547—CAFE MIMOSA
1654—IN THE SHADE OF THE PALMS
1745—NURSE AT NOONGWALLA
1823—ACROSS THE LAGOON
1920—HARBOUR OF DECEIT
1984—THE TENANT OF SAN MATEO
2107—BAMBOO WEDDING
2229—HIDDEN RAPTURE
2460—DREAM ISLAND
2485—DESERT HAVEN
2745—A NIGHT OF THE BEGUINE

# Tempest
# in the Tropics
## Roumelia Lane

# Harlequin Books

### TORONTO • NEW YORK • LONDON
### AMSTERDAM • PARIS • SYDNEY • HAMBURG
### STOCKHOLM • ATHENS • TOKYO • MILAN

Original hardcover edition published in 1986
by Mills & Boon Limited

ISBN 0-373-02834-2

Harlequin Romance first edition May 1987

Printed in U.S.A.

# CHAPTER ONE

THE raft was ready. In the clearing of the tropical rain forest Lindsey explained how it must be transported to the river. Hot and sticky, she ran a hand beneath her swathe of fair hair and spared a glance for the tall, lean stranger over by the trading store.

She had sensed his mildly startled reaction as his eyes had come to rest on her. She knew he was taking in the curving outline of her breasts beneath her khaki shirt, her slim brown legs in brief shorts.

If she hadn't been so keyed up with the job in hand she might have allowed herself the usual wry amusement. She was accustomed to men coming to these parts and registering this kind of veiled surprise; a girl like her, surrounded by Amerindians out here in the wilds of Guyana!

But the raft had now been hoisted on to the shoulders of a dozen or more of the stocky, coffee-coloured natives. She intended to follow it every step of the way to see that nothing went wrong.

Treading in its wake through the trees, nobody knew better than Lindsey how much depended on the outcome of this venture. If she could sail the raft over the silt and the mud bars hereabouts she could convince her father that his logging business would survive up-river.

She had to do something. Dad was just about at the end of his tether. The Davis Logging Company was on the verge of ruin. His lands near the coast were exhausted of timber.

The river Wairuni was erratic and broken by shallow rapids, but she had always felt that the logs would float down easy enough to the main camp. Today she meant to prove it.

The Indians set the raft down beside the river. Lindsey climbed aboard to get the feel of the craft. There was a stout rail midway which she could hold on to.

She felt pleased and confident until she turned and saw the lean stranger draped against a greenheart tree. 'It's none of my business,' he said, 'but might I ask what you're doing?'

She didn't like the critical way he eyed the platform of logs. She liked even less his lazy, superior air as though he was an authority on home made rafts.

'As you said, it's none of your business,' she replied. She gave a sign to the four Indians she had chosen to accompany her. While operations were being put into practice to get the raft down the bank the stranger pushed away from the tree. 'You're not planning to put that thing on water, are you?' His blue gaze sharpened.

'That *is* the idea,' she said coolly. 'It doesn't have wheels, as you can see.'

She hoped her sarcasm would put him off. It didn't. He came forward to say curtly, 'I'm new to these parts but I've studied information on the Wairuni river. It's tricky.'

Typical! Only just arrived and telling *her* what to do!

'Well, I've been here a long time,' she smiled thinly, 'and I know that the river is quite navigable as far as I'm going. Now if you don't mind.'

The raft floated superbly. Her four assistants climbed aboard. They pushed away from the side and she didn't glance back.

It was only when they had gone several yards that she

became irritatedly aware that the tall stranger was matching the raft's pace with his long strides. 'I suppose you know,' he called over the water, 'that there are rapids at Mazapa creek and the Berera junction?'

'Yes, I know, and goodbye.' She eyed the way ahead and forgot the man.

The motion was exhilarating; fast but not unnervingly so. There were rocky flows and silt patches and the raft skimmed happily along as she had known it would. The true test would be when the gradient lessened and they reached the area where the mud and silt had built up, just past Mazapa creek.

For half an hour she watched how the thonged logs rose and fell over the most formidable obstacles. She had no worries. The timber from the reserves on this southern belt of Davis property could be transported down river. Of this she was completely sure.

Even the Indians had enjoyed the ride. But their grins disappeared when they saw the Mazapa rapids.

Lindsey was looking beyond the boiling waters and feeling elated. The silt bar awaiting them was nothing to what they had sailed over on the run down. And this was the river at its lowest. The rainy season was still some weeks away.

She had no special qualms about the rapids. They looked menacing, but the frothing waters made a cushion over the rocks.

She was amazed when the Indians began to jabber worriedly among themselves. With petrified looks in the direction of the foaming currents they dropped their poles one by one and promptly dived over the side.

'Come back, you idiots!' Lindsey called. 'I've tested the depth between the boulders. The water wouldn't come up to your knees!'

All she got for her pleas was the sight of four pairs of

brown arms and legs threshing wildly en route to the nearest bank.

Resignedly she applied herself to the task of going on alone. With no one to steer now she had to hold on tight to the central bar. The river narrowed towards the rapids, but this would prevent her slewing off course. Once over the silt bar it was clear going all the way down to the saw mill.

In contrast to the roaring foam ahead the water here was deep and almost stagnant. There was green slime floating on the surface. It was only towards the centre where little eddies indicated the build-up of pressure.

Lindsey waited for the raft to be taken into the current. She was surprised how easy it had all been. She was picturing her father's face when she told him of her experiment. Then it happened. Something came crashing down heavily beside her from the bank above.

The raft shuddered. Shock dulled her senses. The next thing she knew she was struggling deep down in the water with a pair of powerful arms battling to hold her.

Naturally she fought like a wild-cat. Not through fear—there was nothing rough about the hands trying to grapple with her—but pure, unadulterated anger. She had come all this way to be deprived of her triumph on this final stretch. The raft would have gone on without her, and confound this bungler, she couldn't even get a view of how it had fared over the silt bar!

Gaspingly she came to the surface—or was hoisted there by the sheer willpower of her assailant. One look at those chiselled, weathered features and she was struggling furiously again. She might have guessed! The know-it-all stranger.

Flailing and choking for breath, she had only one aim left; to break free of his exasperating hold on her and she didn't care if she drowned in the attempt.

She almost did.

Some minutes later, seeing nothing but a red haze beneath her lowered lashes she felt herself being transported against a hard chest through the shallows. By the time they reached the bank she had recovered sufficient strength to fight wildly in the steely arms that held her.

On being put down on firm ground she found enough breath to demand blazingly, 'Would you mind telling me what you're playing at?'

Hunched over, gulping in lungs full of air, his reply was hoarse. 'You damned near drowned us both out there. I ought to toss you back in the river and let you follow your toy boat over the rapids.'

Toy boat! All her work and careful planning. She was so angry she wanted to hit him. If she had known him a little better she would have done.

He recovered slowly. His khaki shirt and slacks clung to his lean frame. Straightening he spoke between his teeth, 'What in hell's name do you use for brains, queening it on a thrown-together raft! Didn't you know it would be liable to break up like matchwood on those rocks?'

'Maybe it has,' Lindsey said serenely. If the logs had got through what else mattered?

'You are definitely kinky,' he decided. His glance trailed over her. Colouring, she realised that her clothes were clinging to her in much the same way as his. She also saw, looking down, that the top button of her shirt had pulled away in the struggle, showing a fair portion of lacy bra. Distastefully she scooped out a length of green slime.

'If we're going to avoid going down with the fever we'd better get out of these wet things.' He began to move through the trees. 'My jeep's out on the track.'

'Go ahead.' Airily she remained where she was. 'I'll make my own way back to the trading store.'

He turned, looked at her for a moment and shrugged. 'Suit yourself.'

When he had disappeared through the trees some of her bravado left her. The tropical forest became somehow ominous without his presence. The cries of birds and animals, which she had barely noticed before, now sounded distinctly menacing. She recalled that the trading store was several miles up river. The evening breeze blew decidedly chilly over her wet skin.

When she arrived at the jeep its owner had a fire going. Stripped to the waist, he had pegged his shirt on a make-shift line and was now preparing to do the same with his drill slacks.

'Er!' She announced her presence in a horrified voice and was relieved when he jerked a blanket out of the jeep and draped it around his middle.

He took a second one and tossed it to her.

'Here. You'll find a can of fresh water at the back of the jeep. Rinse out your stuff and I'll peg them alongside mine.'

Just like that! Fuming afresh, she advanced. 'Having toppled me from my only transport, I should think you would have the decency to drive me back to the trading store.'

Tucking in his blanket sarong-like at the waist, he stooped to the rear-view mirror and proceeded to run a comb through his hair. 'I don't figure on going any place for some time,' he said.

She stared at him, nervously aware of their darkening surroundings, 'You . . . don't mean you're planning to stay here . . . for the night?'

He nodded. 'I'm used to camping out. I've got food and water and two blankets—well I had two blankets, but now you're here you'll have to roll yourself in one till morning.'

At this Lindsey let out an angry exclamation. 'If you think I'm going to bed down beside you, you're crazy!'

He tossed aside the comb and moved in on the spot where she stood dripping. Hypnotised by his threatening air, she noticed wildly how the column of hair snaking up from his navel fanned out into a mahogany-dark fuzz on his chest. 'I risked my neck scooping you off a death-trap of a raft,' he bit out. 'I don't intend to have you dying on my hands of fever after all my trouble. Now, are you going to stop making out like a tug-boat prima donna and start peeling off those wet things, or do I do it myself?'

Lindsey shrank behind the back of the jeep and hurriedly began to undo the remaining buttons of her shirt. He had said he was new to these parts. Whoever he was, he had a nasty, authoritative manner.

Stripping, she raised her voice to make her resentment known. 'You had a nerve poking your nose in my affairs,' she called. 'For your information I know this river better than any newcomer around here. And I was all set for easily skimming the rapids till you ruined everything.'

'You might have made it with your crew.' There was a rattle of utensils. 'Alone, you didn't stand a chance.'

'I don't know why the Indians should take a fright,' she scoffed. 'They've seen rapids before.'

'But not afloat a matchstick platform which was hardly the *Kon-tiki*.' She hated the satire in his voice.

'The Indians are good at building rafts,' she asserted, swishing her clothes round vengefully in the water and wringing them out.

'The Indians are good at a variety of tasks. Splicing together rotting timber and making it river-worthy is not one of them,' came the dry reply.

Tucking in the blanket beneath her armpits—well she could hardly sport it at the waist as he was doing—she came out from behind the jeep. 'To say you're a stranger to the place you haven't wasted much time in summing up the local populace,' she jeered.

'I said I was new to these surroundings, not to the country.' He was turning out a tin of stew into a billy-can over the fire.

She ignored the make-shift line and went to drape her wet things over a clump of bushes near the track. Noting how the latter twisted away through the forest she smiled with malicious satisfaction. 'You must have had a tortuous drive keeping up with the raft. I can't think why you didn't end up wrapped round a tree.'

'I wasn't trailing you,' he said deflating her ego. 'I was finishing a job of work when I saw you and your trusty band heading for the creek,' the satire again was obvious.

'It's a pity you didn't stick to your own business and leave me to attend to mine.' Every time she thought of how close she had come to proving that timber would float down river, she blazed afresh at this man's interference.

The stew smelled good, but she would rather die than let him see she was affected by the aroma. Picking a spot well away from him, but close enough to sneak a little warmth from the fire, she perched on a rock and sat rigidly, her face averted.

She heard him helping himself to the stew. In between mouthfuls he said 'What was the idea of risking your neck on the raft anyway? I can't imagine you were doing it for a bet. Women are lousy gamblers. They never pay up when they lose.'

'Oh?' She treated him to an arch look. 'And are we to assume that you're as much an authority on the opposite sex as you are on the idiosyncracies of the River Wairuni?'

'I've been around,' he smacked his lips over the stew.

Annoyed at her rumbling stomach, she spoke up with renewed dislike. 'Well, in the first place you can stop dramatising my trip on the raft. I knew perfectly well what I was doing. In the second place, I don't have to explain my actions to some ... some hobo in the forest.'

He scraped every last vestige of stew from his tin plate and then went to pour fresh water for washing up. Later the rich tantalising smell of coffee reached her averted nostrils. She concentrated on the scenery, but was not much cheered. Darkness was drawing in rapidly over the forest. What stars there were, were barely visible through the matted greenery above. Her four Indian companions would be now well on their way back to the trading store.

A sudden gust of wind lifted her clothes from the bushes. They ended up decorating the ground around the fire. She rose hurriedly to grab at them. The more so because the hobo type was bent on the same purpose. In her haste to reach them first she forgot her ungainly gown, the blanket. The next second she would have gone sprawling but for the speed with which he reached her. She felt a complete fool being steadied by him, especially as her bare arms and shoulders came into contact with his taut physique. His skin was warm, and she shivered. She caught a glimpse of his profile in the firelight, copper-coloured and rough-hewn. Her own pale hair draped in polished strands over one muscular brown shoulder.

'You're just about the most cussed female I ever ran into,' he growled, standing her on her feet. 'I don't aim to be saddled with you any longer than I can help, so like I said, we'll put your things on the line where they'll dry.'

Furiously she had to stand by and watch while he clipped each item painstakingly alongside his own. How she wished she had been a little more conservative in her choice of underwear today! Doll-pink lace looked ludicrous between his brown fingers.

She went back to her rock perch with as much dignity as she could muster under the circumstances. Some time later she heard him banking up the fire and preparing to bed down for the night.

A chill crept over her skin. She tucked the blanket up to her chin and tried to relax on the uncomfortable rock. It seemed awfully dark when one looked away from the fire.

'Er ... isn't it a little early to go to sleep?' she asked shakily.

'I've had a long, hard day,' he said drowsily.

'But ... but ...' She sought around frantically in her mind for a topic of conversation. 'I ... don't know who you are ...'

'Mackenzie,' he yawned comfortably. 'Brance Mackenzie.'

She had noticed his pronounced drawl from the start. She said now, 'You're an American, aren't you?'

'Canadian,' he corrected from inside his blanket.

'Same thing,' she shrugged.

'To anyone but a Canadian.' The voice rallied and had a metallic thread.

She had an idea she had offended his national pride with her remark. She felt good. The way he had ruined her carefully planned exercise on the river, he deserved to suffer a knock or two in return. She wished she could think up more ways of getting at him.

'There's a place called Mackenzie sixty-seven miles

up the Demerera river. It's just a bauxite town,' she said more to demonstrate her knowledge of the country. Annoyingly, she couldn't think of anything more derogatory to say at the moment.

'There's a lot of us around.' She felt that he smiled sleepily. His breathing became deep, inclined to be rhythmical.

He hadn't asked about her, which left her feeling a little peevish.

'I'm . . . English,' she offered in a brusque attempt to keep him awake.

'I didn't need to hear your Tunbridge Wells accent to figure that out.' The voice was thick with sleep, yet there was no mistaking the irony there.

'I hope you're not going to trot out that old chestnut "mad dogs and Englishmen",' she said in bored tones.

'I was thinking more of mad females and floppy rafts.'

Oh of course he would have to get *that* in.

She made an acid response, but knew before the words had left her lips, that he was sound asleep.

For some time she had had her eyes fixed on the stew pan near the red embers of the fire. Now she crept close and saw there was a good portion idling there. She moved furtively around and having located plate and spoon and some chunks of bread sat down and ate hungrily. The coffee, for afters, tasted divine. She was just draining the last delicious dregs when the screech of monkeys squabbling for the best night perch made her tense. Now that her greed was satisfied she was once again aware of the darkness beyond the fire. The thought of huge lizards roaming nearby made her flesh creep. To say nothing of tree-frogs, coral snakes and predatory four-footed animals.

A sudden high-pitched cackle made her drop her tin

mug and leap in the direction of the figure stretched out near the fire. 'Er . . . Mr Mackenzie . . . Brance . . .' she croaked urgently. Log-like, the blanketed shape didn't even stir ar her quaking entreaty.

Nervously she backed away from the encroaching perimeter of trees almost tumbling over his prone body in her confusion. She sat down with a bump, just missing his lap, and eyed the darkness which seemed alive with moving shapes. At least with him at her back nothing could creep up on her from behind!

Relaxing in the warmth of the fire she mused drowsily on anything that came into her mind rather than admit, even grudgingly, that his presence was comforting.

When she awoke the pale light of dawn was filtering down through the trees. She realised that her back prop had gone and that she was lying snuggled up comfortably against the blanketed shape. Horrified, she felt for her own blanket and was relieved to find that it was tucked round her. She saw, slanting her eyes without moving her head, that the fire had been stoked up through the night. She saw also that her clothes had been rescued from the dawn damp and were neatly folded in a pile beside the fire.

Indignantly she moved away from the slumbering figure and stealthily grabbed them. It took her only a minute or so to get dressed. During this time her mind was busy.

If she had her bearings right, this track linked up about half a mile north from here with the main route to the trading store. Danny Capucho, part owner and a friend of hers, would be making the return trip from town any time now. She could thumb a lift.

After a brief look around the campsite, lingering only long enough to cast a disdainful glance towards the long, recumbent figure in the blanket, she turned and slipped away.

The trading store was on the outskirts of one of the Amerindian villages in the bush. Here the river was lined by lush green forest. Stilt-legged pink flamingoes graced the shallows. Other bright river birds cast jewelled tints over the water.

Lindsey thanked Danny for the lift and climbed into her own transport, a rickety logging runabout parked near the store. When she got down to the saw mill past Mazapa rapids she parked momentarily and went to look at the river. Her heart leapt when she saw that the raft had made it and was caught between rushes and flotsam at the side of the mill.

Eyeing its battered appearance she had a couple of sober moments, but these were quickly dispersed when she realised that she now had exciting news for her father.

Or was it?

He did not dance round the living room at Springlands, as she had expected, when she told him.

'You say you've seen logs float down from as far south as the Cacucho trading store? How'd they get in the river?' He eyed her suspiciously.

'Oh, just a little experiment I made,' she shrugged off the details, hoping he wouldn't probe. 'The main thing is we *can* float our timber down to the main saw-mill. And that means that the Davis Logging Company is still very much a thriving concern.'

He ignored her enthusiasm. His manner was more reprehending than congratulatory as he said, 'I hope you haven't been tampering with anything dangerous, Lindy. I know you can be a determined little cuss when you get an idea in your head.'

'Why should you think that?' she asked with some irritation. Her wonderful news appeared to be becoming bogged down in interrogative issues.

'You didn't come home all night for one thing—yes, I know I've only just got back from my trip to Georgetown, but Zina told me she hadn't seen you since yesterday morning at breakfast.'

'Well, I simply took advantage of your absence to make a trip up-river. I sort of got caught up with things latish at Mazapa creek.' *Wasn't that the truth!* 'When it started to get dark I decided to . . . stay there the night.'

'At the saw-mill?'

'Well, not exactly.' She couldn't mention the interfering Brance Mackenzie without having to reveal that she had been actually afloat the raft, so she improvised with, 'I had a fire and food.' She hurried on to implore, 'But why are we wasting time with small talk? With all the southern belt open to us it means there'll be Davis timber for years and years!'

There was no immediate reply. The thick-set figure with greying hair and features toughened by years of back-breaking toil, turned instead to stare out of the window.

If anyone asked, Ben Davis would describe himself as a man who had knocked about the world all his life. Fifteen years ago, he had been left valuable timber reserves in the will of an obscure relative whose descendants dated back to the first British colony settlement in Guyana, in the mid-seventeenth century. Stout, adaptable and hardworking, Ben had taken to the logging business like an old hand. He had dispensed with outdated methods. Profits had grown until soaring inflation meant that more timber had to be felled for the same returns. Now, hope of recouping precious funds sunk into the business to modernise grew slimmer with every day.

He turned from the window and said at last, 'The loan I went to try and arrange in Georgetown didn't come off.'

Lindsey all but laughed her puzzlement. 'Do we need to worry about that now after my news? The way we're placed, we'll be the ones to be offering the loans.'

'It's not news to me, Lindy. I've known that timber could be floated down that stretch of river all along.' His weary reply took her completely by surprise.

'You have?' She blinked. 'But you always told me it was a geographic impossibility.'

'There are obstacles,' he nodded. 'We do, however, have the machinery to take care of those problems.'

'Then why——?' While Lindsey was recalling with no scant annoyance all the work she had put in to prove a useless point, Ben managed a smile. It was a tender, sad smile.

'I've never intended working the timber on the southern stretch,' he said. 'Your mother had a rough time of it when she was alive, seeing little of me in the years that we were married. I want things to be different for you, Lindy. When I go those rich reserves will belong to you.'

'Dad!' Lindsey gave a little cry and ran to him. 'You're not saying that you've been holding on to all that precious timber just for me! Why, the region's vast. Besides it doesn't make sense trying to borrow money when you have those kind of assets.'

'It does to me.' He stroked her hair. 'Just now money buys very little, but in the years to come when the economy's more stable, you'll have a fortune in timber.'

'And what do we do in the meantime?' she twinkled at him sternly. 'You have a business to run. And I'm your second-in-command, remember? I think I've learned plenty about logging in the time I've been here, don't you?'

'I reckon you'll be able to take over when I retire,' he acknowledged with a grin.

'And when will that be?' she scoffed. 'You've only just turned a very active sixty. It will be another ten years before you even start thinking about putting your lumberjack boots away.'

Though he looked as though he might agree with this, that worried frown flickered across his brow again. 'Maybe not,' he sighed. 'Most of our land's bled dry, Lindy. And the creditors don't wait for transplanted trees to mature.'

'But I can,' she said sweetly. 'So why don't we do a swop? I'll work the sapling country when you retire and we'll shift our work-force to the southern reaches right away.'

'Now, girl,' he wagged an admonishing finger at her. 'None of your pushy ways. I knew you'd try something like this if you ever found out about that stretch of river.'

'It was wicked of you to fob me off with that tale about silt bars,' she scolded smilingly.

'I might have known you'd find out for yourself,' he scowled, though there was pride and admiration in the way he said it. The next moment he was adamant again. 'I've set aside the lands on our southern boundary to swell your inheritance, and I'm not going to budge from that.'

'The only inheritance I care about is you and me being happy together,' she snuggled against his chest.

'It won't always be you and me.' He squinted at her significantly, blustering on at her blank look, 'Well, one day you'll be thinking of getting wed. Then you'll have a husband and maybe raise sons for the business.'

'Twenty-two is not exactly ancient,' she said humorously. 'And to be honest I've never given marriage a thought.'

'Well, most of the men around here have,' he said succinctly. 'I've seen the way they look at you, Lindy. You've grown into an attractive young woman. Mollenda has mentioned the fact to me more than once these past weeks.'

Nicholas Mollenda, the son of the family who owned the estate next to Springlands. Lindsey wrinkled her nose. 'Nick's all right,' she said, 'but I've never viewed him as a prospective husband.'

She found their neighbour friendly and charming, but hardly overpowering. Curiously the image of him moved her even less just now. Quickly, as though afraid to pursue this line of thought, she added, 'You're the only man in my life. Now why don't we stop digressing and get down to making plans for opening up the new reserves? I know there's still a few miles to go on Tacana Hill, but you could get Sam Jensen and his crew on to——'

'Lin-dy,' Ben growled reprovingly. To no avail.

She eyed him blandly. 'What will you do when you've no wood to cut?' she asked. 'You'll be miserable. You're like a tetchy toucan when you're not working. And I'd be miserable because you're miserable. Is that what you want? Admit it. You're itching to get working in the southern forests.'

'Well I—dammit no!' He caught himself up in time. 'That section of the Davis terrain I'm willing to you. I promised myself.' But Lindsey knew she had touched a yearning in him.

'If we line up those valuable tracts of timber ready for moving in after Tacana Hill,' she pushed home, 'the Davis Logging Company will be a humming concern again. And I certainly don't want that kind of inheritance if you're going to die out of boredom.'

'Lindy,' he groaned. 'You're the doggonest female for convincing a man against his will.'

'How long will it take you to drive out and weigh up that section of country?' she put the question.

Caught off guard he replied, 'I could be up there by twelve.' And eagerly, forgetting his adamant stand now, 'It's thick with hardwoods—acapu, amarelo, and jarana going on for three hundred feet tall.'

'Well, what are you waiting for?' She laughed. 'And you can bring me back some slipper orchids. They'll look well on the table tonight at dinner.'

He moved rapidly towards the door, but not without a disapproving air accompanying his high spirits. 'If you weren't so darned grown up I'd put you over my knee. But by God I feel good when I think of all that virgin timber just waiting for the saw.'

After she had waved him off, Lindsey strolled in the open. Springlands, the Davis residence, was a wooden structure set amid tall trees on the edge of open grassland. Its grounds were spacious, but inclined to be a little unkempt. Blossoming tropical shrubs mingled with thickets of small trees and lawned stretches were patchy and starred with forest wild flowers. But Lindsey loved the place.

Ever since her father had invited her out here at seventeen when she had found herself alone in the world, she had revelled in the open-air life. Ben had overlooked her sex after the first impact of meeting a leggy girl with pale, unformed features. It had pleased him to discover she had spirit and before long he was teaching her the logging business as he might have done a son of his.

Shyness at first had created a distance between them, but with time his daughter had come to mean the world to Ben. Lindsey loved her father deeply.

She plucked at a shrub in passing, with a happy glow now. They had successfully bridged the crisis in their lives. It was just like Ben to think only of her in the midst of trouble, but she had decided that they should weather this thing together and she was glad that he had agreed.

A week later, she was seeing for herself what a treasure of timber there was in the southlands. Wandering at the fringe of the great forests was awe-inspiring. Men and machines were clearing the dense undergrowth. Over pungent-smelling ground in their wake she picked her way between magnificent specimens, thick-boled and towering to make a matted green roof high overhead.

She had come dressed for the rough outdoors. Her safari shirt and matching slacks were belted in at the waist. While being worn for the express purpose of preventing her clothes from flapping and catching on thorns, the leather belt, at the same time, emphasised the curve of her breasts and shapely hips. She had pinned up her pale shoulder-length hair into an unruly cluster on top of her head. This revealed a vulnerable curve of throat and jaw-line.

Her attention was proudly on the trees as she moved at the edge of these miles and miles of rolling forest. All this was Springfields properly, bequeathed with the house and vast tracts east of the river to Ben Davis by a distant second cousin.

She came to the logging camp office, a crude hut erected on the cleared site. Her father was at the door issuing instructions to Sam, his chief logger. Something in his manner, and the way Sam looked at him in blank amazement before hurrying off to do his bidding, caused her a momentary qualm. Was something wrong? On a perfect day like this with all the forest to go at, she couldn't imagine what.

Ben turned and saw her. It was then that she noticed

the pallor of his features; the look of complete despair stamped there.

'Dad!' She hurried forward, her heart missing a beat. 'Has something happened? One of the machines . . .?'

'No, nothing's happened,' he gave her a ghastly smile. 'And nothing's going to happen. No wood-cutting for sure.'

'But . . . what . . . Have the men refused to work?'

'Have you ever known them to be anything but keen as mustard?' His smile sagged. It disappeared completely as he told her, 'We're up against a ban, Lindy. Not one single tree can be felled.'

'On whose orders?' Her breathing quickened.

'Some organisation carrying government backing.' Lindsey gathered that his attitude was linked with a presence inside the hut. Whoever was in there was responsible for the aged, beaten look on her father's face. This was enough to send her marching in, bosom heaving.

Though she entered breathing fire, she did pause briefly in surprise, her pulses fluttering annoyingly, when she saw Brance Mackenzie standing there. Shirt-sleeves rolled up showing muscle-threaded brown arms, khaki slacks sitting on lean hips, he was jotting something in a notebook. Having seen her through the open doorway his own surprise had had time to evaporate. With hardly a glance her way, he drawled, 'Well, if it isn't the river-boat queen!'

She retaliated with, 'Not you again!'

'You might have let me know you were leaving.' There was a curtness in his manner.

'I'm not aware that I have to answer to you for my movements.'

Ben looked from one to the other, his bewilderment obvious. 'Do you two know each other?'

'He tried something of the same high-handed tactics on me, when I met him up river last week,' Lindsey said sketchily. And before either could reply, 'Would you mind telling me what you're doing on Davis property?'

He flicked his book shut, tucked it in his back pocket and shrugged, 'I've explained it all to your father, but if you want it in simple terms it goes like this ... You may have heard about the growing world concern regarding the destruction of forests. Clearance of tree belts causes erosion of soil, rain sweeps down treeless valleys and in many cases floods follow.'

'You're talking about clearing trees to yield arable land surely,' Lindsey said hotly. 'Whereas we re-plant once we have cleared a forest.' A little guiltily, she said nothing about their having only just started this practice in the last two or three years.

'This is only part of the problem,' the forestry man went on. 'There's the genetic loss as well. Of the thousands of plants known to science, two-thirds, many of which are valuable in the medical field, grow in the tropics and are threatened with extinction.'

'Are you telling me that we're involved in an argument for wild plant conservation?' Lindsey tried to sneer. It didn't quite come off because, drat the man, she knew that he was talking sense. How many times had she privately bemoaned the fact that resplendent trees must fall, that delicate forest flora must disappear beneath the ruthless penetration into the interior? To justify this encroaching desolation she snapped, 'We do have a living to earn.'

'You're entitled to that,' he acknowledged. 'But I've been making a tour of the Davis lands. The organisation I work for has a rule. No property may divest itself of more than half of its natural forest reserves, and you've gone way over that.'

'And if we choose to ignore this rule?' she flung up her head.

He lifted his shoulders. 'I've heard that the fines outweigh any profits that might be made.'

Lindsey resisted the urge, for the second time since knowing him, to wipe that self-assured look off his face with the force of her hand. 'We're not just going to take this, you know,' she said quiveringly. 'We've got lawyers . . .'

'We're trying to influence South American nations on the need for conservation. The Guyana authorities are willing to co-operate.' As though this spoke for itself he added, 'Is there nothing else you could do? Farming or——'

'Save your sympathy,' she cut him off. 'And now that you've delivered your shabby bit of news there's nothing to keep you, is there?'

A metallic glint—was it of anger? she hoped— appeared in his eyes at her peremptory dismissal. Conversely there was something mildly mocking in his manner as he viewed her steamed-up mood. Ignoring her then, he passed on and said, 'I'm sorry to have to be the bearer of this kind of ultimatum, Mr Davis. If there's anything I can do to assist you in any way, please let me know. I'll be taking samples locally so I'll be around for a while.'

He thrust out a hand. Ben took it in his own and smiled in a dazed way, 'Thanks.'

When he had left, Lindsey wailed in disgust. 'Did you have to be polite to that man! As for shaking his hand . . .'

'He's only doing his job, Lindy,' Ben sighed. 'Like we do ours.'

'Like we're *going to continue doing ours*,' she corrected grimly. 'I suppose you'll be taking it up with the lawyers straight away?'

'This afternoon,' he nodded. 'But they're not likely to know of a loophole in something as powerfully sewn up as this.'

'Well, badger them to find one!' she cried tremulously. 'I'd rather die than let that odious Brance Mackenzie have the last word round here!'


## CHAPTER TWO

THE next three days were the longest Lindsey had lived through. While Ben made trips back and forth into town, she hung around the house waiting anxiously for his return. When she could no longer tolerate the inactivity she helped Zina, their housemaid with the chores, or half-heartedly tidied up the stretches of garden.

On the third afternoon she was there to see her father's ranch-waggon enter the front gate. She knew by his face that they had lost.

'It's no go, Lindy,' he said, following her into the living-room. 'They say we haven't a thing with which we could make a stand against an outfit like Mackenzie's. And even if they agreed to, I haven't got that kind of fee.'

Lindsey asked through white lips, 'Is that it? Is there nothing we can do?'

'I suppose the man's done us a favour in a way,' Ben's tired voice was half humorous. 'At least you'll have that inheritance I planned for you now.'

'Dad, you can't mean that!' Lindsey was quietly aghast. 'This is the death-knell to the Davis Logging Company. You know it is.'

'We've still got Tacana Hill,' he brightened only fractionally. 'I believe Mackenzie did some wrangling to get us that.'

'With all the harm he's done us, he owes us more than Tacana Hill,' she scoffed bitterly. 'A few weeks' work, then what will we do?'

'We'll think of something.' He looked at the position of the sun in the sky through the window and added, 'I'd better be getting over to the southlands to give Sam a hand with running the camp down. In the week we were on the site we've accumulated an awful lot of gear.'

'All those men and machines we moved in. All for nothing,' she blazed softly.

'It's not the end of the world.' He patted her shoulder encouragingly in passing. But as Lindsey watched her father move defeatedly from the room she knew it was the end of his.

She waited only long enough to let him get a few miles' start on the road, then she climbed into her own logging runabout. *She* didn't intend to calmly obey overbearing forestry officials. Brance Mackenzie was going to learn that there was one person at Springlands who was prepared to fight this thing every inch of the way.

When she arrived at the logging site, she could hear the shouts of the men re-loading heavy tools and equipment. She was gripped by a momentary bleakness, but this didn't concern her now.

She struck out into the forest away from the activity. Though she was looking for a certain lean figure she couldn't help noticing the wealth of plant life underfoot: pink bells in emerald rosettes, blue and yellow clusters on veined green and a myriad flesh-leaved specimens.

She came upon a wooden cabin which didn't improve her temper. Making himself at home on *their* property!

The door was open. Unhesitatingly, she stormed inside.

The comfort of the place rattled her even further. There was a camp bed neatly made up in one corner. Shelves were stacked with groceries, and a stove for warmth added—the nerve of it!—a homely touch. But it was the long trestle table under the window on which she set her sights. Not just because it was filled with rows and rows of glass jars, some already labelling their contents. It was the figure stooping over to examine one of them on which she bore down.

Her breathing was so rapid she could hardly speak. With an effort at control, she managed to say tightly, 'Has anyone ever told you it's an offence to squat on private property?'

He raised himself as though her irate entry was not wholly unexpected. 'Still sizzling because your logging lease has run out?'

'Oh, you know how to put it obliquely, don't you?' she sneered. 'There's no mention of insufferable forestry types nosing where they're not wanted. If you hadn't come here we would be well on our way with felling timber on the new site.'

'That's right.'

His detached air incensed her. 'They're our trees, you know. What business is it of yours what we do with them?'

'I happen to believe in the conservation of natural forests.'

'And what about us logging people? We can lose our livelihood and starve so long as your precious trees are left standing. Or perhaps you'd like to put us in your little jars too and study us.'

He turned lazily from the table. His look was unmistakably mocking as he eyed her open-necked shirt, belted safari slacks and the wholly feminine, palpitating form beneath. 'I hardly think you come under the tree species,' he drawled.

Something in his gaze unsteadied her. She felt her pulses quicken and blustered, 'Well, you may have put a stop for the moment to the wood-cutting programme hereabouts, but your precious "organisation" authority gives you no right to set youself up in the ... the botanical business,' she waved an arm at the jars, 'on Springlands property.'

'Your father has given me permission to work here.' She was stunned at this news, but by no means bereft of a reply. 'Oh, I see! You practice a little blackmail by offering Dad the go-ahead on Tacana Hill so that you can settle yourself in nice and cosy here.'

She had seen the way the brown jaw could flex on more than one occasion. This time, as she was not standing in dripping wet clothes, she was not intimidated by it. 'Well as you're not all that quick to take a hint this ought to show you that I, for one, don't intend to stand by and let you make a fool out of my father.'

She raised an arm to sweep the whole lot of glass jars on to the floor. A red hot pain shot down her wrist as he grabbed it. 'Get your bitchy little hands off those specimens!'

He jerked her away from the table and against him with a force that left her breathless. She fought wildly to free herself from his vice-like arms. Hatingly, after several tempestuous moments, she had to cede to his strength. While she glowered, panting for breath, he eyed her narrowly, and with a detestable superior smile. 'You've got all the spirit of a huffy tree shrew,' he growled. 'How long have you lived in these surroundings?'

'Since I was seventeen,' she flung up her head to blaze at him. 'And it will take more than you and your flower-picking fancies to tell me what to do.'

'Want to bet?' His fingers sunk into her flesh beneath the stuff of her shirt, telling her that she had both angered and inflamed him with her biting scorn. 'I wouldn't mind taming you.' Her soft curves crushed against his hard frame, he made the most of her proximity. 'It would give me the greatest pleasure to break some of that flouncy temperament in you.'

'You're good at throwing your weight about, aren't you?' she jeered to hide the acceleration of her heartbeats. 'You almost drowned me on the raft just to prove your superlative brawn.'

'You'd have been lucky to come out of that little venture in one piece.'

'Then you forced me to spend the dark hours at your fireside while you calmly bedded down for the night.'

'You didn't do too badly yourself. When I woke up to think about putting wood on the fire you were curled up like a harmless kitten against me with your claws nicely sheathed.'

'I've got more than claws,' she flashed. 'I can bite too.'

'I bet you can.' His grip was merciless. 'Though you looked helpless enough when I tucked your blanket around you.'

Her cheeks flamed when she recalled that that had been her total garment at the fireside.

Pleased that he had unsteadied her virtuous self-esteem he murmured, his gaze speaking volumes, 'I could have extracted payment for saving you from an untimely end on that raft.' His face was so close to hers she could see the flecks in his blue eyes. And much, much more.

In spite of her fury, a rich, excitable warmth coursed along her veins. She had been battling not just to rid herself of his arms, but against a suffocatingly pleasurable flame which his nearness ignited in her. Now, something in her mesmerised by his look, she melted unknowingly against him, her lips slightly parted, her eyes starred with both anger and expectation.

The hard smile on his lips giving way to something intense in his eyes, his mouth came down. It stopped mid-way as the raucous sound of a klaxon filled the air.

Lindsey went rigid in his arms. 'Something's wrong!' She broke free from his embrace. 'I know that sound. There's an emergency at the camp.'

Brance was beside her as she hurried out of the door. They crossed the section of forest together and came upon pandemonium at the logging site. Men were running back and forth. Nobody seemed to have any clear idea of what they were doing. One man was doing his best to come to grips with the situation.

Sam Jensen turned when he saw Lindsey. His grizzled features were putty-coloured. 'We were loading the cross-cut mechanical saw. The engine overbalanced on the ramp . . .'

Lindsey knew that mounted motor, it weighed as much as a small tractor. 'And Dad?' The words were jerked from her by something she saw in Sam's eyes.

'He . . . well he . . .'

'No!' Lindsey fought her way through the circle of men. Brance took her by the shoulders, but not before she had seen the familiar, dear-to-her figure in a twisted position on the ground. His face had a ghastly pallor, but he managed a smile. 'I'm okay, Lindy. The mangy thing toppled just when we had it almost there. I reckon I didn't high-tail it out of the way quick enough.'

Brance weighed up the position of his trapped leg under the bulk of the engine with a brisk order. 'Get the log winch.'

The men seemed to come out of their trance at this grasping of the initiative. Sam brightened as though he ought to have thought of this himself and echoed the order, 'Get the log winch.'

It took only minutes to drive the winch into position. When Ben's leg became visible it was obvious he had lost a considerable amount of blood.

Brance had the men lift him clear in a semi-conscious state. He told Lindsey, 'We'll have to get him straight to town. See if you can round up a logging truck and a clean ground-sheet to lay him on.'

Lindsey went rapidly to do his bidding, not knowing that Brance had got rid of her so that he could inspect the extent of her father's injuries. When she returned he gave her an encouraging look, though his mouth was tight as the lumberjacks gently laid their boss in the back of the truck.

Lindsey ignored her own discomfort on the drive to town. She cradled her father's head on her knee and gritted her teeth at the lack of springs in the truck and the numerous pot-holes in the roads.

The lights were flickering on one by one in Moratica when they arrived. A small community compared to Georgetown on the coast, the jungle foliage gave it a picturesque air. Besides its wooden houses on stilts, it had the usual amenities of a small town, an hotel, a library, and a cottage hospital.

Their stay in the waiting-room while Ben was examined, was to Lindsey interminable. Brance gave her a cigarette and lit it with his own. She smoked absently, her eyes never leaving the swing doors.

At last, after what seemed hours, Doctor Loy, a

friend of her father's, came though. 'It could have been a lot worse, Lindsey,' he smiled. 'A broken leg and a gashed thigh. We've given him the usual precautionary shots. He'll sleep tonight. Tomorrow you can take him home.'

Lindsey's legs almost buckled beneath her with relief. Brance took her arm. 'Let's go and have a meal,' he said. 'We can stay in town overnight and come back in the morning.'

He smiled their thanks to the doctor and led her away. Lindsey was so prostrate with tiredness, she ate the meal placed before her in the hotel dining-room mechanically. The long, gruelling drive to town, the strain of imagining the worst, and then the sudden release from the unbearable tension made everything appear dream-like.

But she rallied when they went out on to the verandah later for a drink, perhaps because it was a beautiful evening, with stars piercing a blue-black sky and the scent of blossoms beyond the verandah filling the air.

Steeling herself against the effect Brance had on her in so dangerous an atmosphere, she swung from viewing the night to say, 'Well now that you've eased your conscience rushing Dad to hospital you must be dying to get back to your bottled posies. Please don't hang about on my account.'

'It's on my account too.' He moved towards her in the shadows. 'I seem to recall we left some unfinished business in the cabin.'

Lindsey saw the queer glint in his eyes at the same moment that his arms closed around her. She shivered at his touch. Never in her life had she known this utterly sweet, melting feeling. But anger came to her aid. 'I haven't the faintest notion what you're talking about,' she lied. 'The only unfinished business I can recall is that I was in the act of kicking you off our land.'

'If you've forgotten so easily, maybe this will jog your memory.' Brutally he planted his lips on hers.

Lindsey's spine turned to water. Strained against his hard frame, the stars she had seen in the heavens seemed to suffuse now inside her brain. Weakened by his nearness, the flame of yearning she had striven to ignore, licked along her veins as his mouth explored hers. It was like battling against an onrushing tide, a surge of overpowering rapture which she had no strength to resist.

'And I was in the act of taming some of that she-cat out of you,' he growled finally, releasing her.

Lindsey was still among the stars when he let her go. To cover her confusion she snapped, 'How dare you add insult to injury by trying to make love to me!'

'You enjoyed every minute of it. Admit it.'

Though her blood was still tingling she flung at him, 'The only thing I enjoy about you is detesting your over-sized ego.'

'Don't think I go a bundle on falling heavily for a bitchy logging woman,' his mouth was tight. 'But we're tinder to each other, you and me. It's not something we're going to be able to wrap up and neatly tuck away out of sight.'

'Nothing would please me more if you would do just that, wrap up and tuck yourself away *a long way from here*,' she said in high-pitched tones. 'But for you, I wouldn't be here. And my father certainly wouldn't be lying in a hospital bed. He's worked all his life in rough conditions. It's worry and strain of your threatening his living that caused him to be careless today. You're crazy if you think I could ever feel any kind of a soft spot for you.'

'No?' He jerked her into his arms. The kiss he gave her was long, demanding and all-consuming for the two of them.

Shaking visibly when he released her she said stiltedly, 'If you don't mind, I think I'll go to my room.'

'A good idea.' His gaze flame-lit and humorous, he stood aside for her to pass.

The next morning Lindsey did all she could to avoid seeing Brance around the hotel until it was time to leave. Then Doctor Loy 'phoned to say that her father was still feeling the effects of sedation and probably wouldn't be mobile until around noon. He suggested that she eat at the hotel and come along to collect him afterwards.

She had no choice but to lunch with Brance. He made no mention of last night. His manner was abrupt to the point of terseness. Eyeing his chiselled features when his gaze was lowered, she experienced a stab of malicious satisfaction. He didn't want to fall in love with her any more than she wanted to fall in love with him!

It was a mood that quickly dissolved into panic and exasperation. Of all the men there were in the world, why did her crazy heart have to go and pick on somebody like Brance MacKenzie? The idea of her feeling anything for the man who had ruined her father's life was unthinkable and impossible. She would rather marry ... well, just anybody before she would admit to any tender thoughts where he was concerned. And she intended to tell herself that at least twenty times a day.

Brance changed completely when they went to pick up her father. He was considerate and cheerful and helped the older man to overcome his plaster-cast disability by assisting him into his seat. Annoyingly, Lindsey was pressed close to Brance as they all squeezed into the cab.

During the drive, the conversation between the two men was amenable, much to Lindsey's disgust. Ben apparently bore no malice towards the man who had put him out of business. Irrationally, though the trees might never be cut down, she guessed that he was content in a way, that she would now have the inheritance he had planned for her. Though Springlands was vast, most of it had been worked and the land itself would produce no income as it was.

Ben, always energetic in body and spirit, was already making plans for some other form of income from the barren stretches.

'You're going to have to rest up for a while,' Lindsey cut into the conversation firmly. 'Doctor Loy suggests at least three days in bed to give those stitches time to knit.'

'Now don't go making an invalid out of me, Lindy,' Ben complained. 'A busted leg is no reason to stay laid up, and besides, Sam's getting on in years. Who's going to see to the clearance of all that logging machinery if I don't get over to the new site and give him a hand to keep the men on the job? They're keen to cut trees, but they're not too happy at being told to pack up when they've only just arrived.'

'Lindsey's right, Ben,' Brance said, swinging the wheel. 'You're not as young as you were. If you want to be using that leg as good as new in a few weeks, you'll have to rest it up now to allow it time to heal.'

'You may be right, Brance,' he conceded heavily, 'but I'm a working man, remember. I've got responsibilities that don't get any lighter just because I'm temporarily at the mercy of a crutch.'

'Okay, forget your worries about shifting the rest of that logging equipment. As I'm on the spot I'll keep an eye on the men myself. And there can't be anything else pressing at the moment. If there is, just give me the word and——'

'In case you've both forgotten,' Lindsey broke in icily, 'I happen to work for the Davis Logging Company too, and when the head of the firm is indisposed, I make the decisions.'

'You're not intending to leave me lying all on my own in the house are you, Lindy?' Ben asked slyly. He obviously preferred Brance substituting for him where the men were concerned.

But she was pleased to know that he had seen sense at last. 'You mean you're going to take the doctor's advice, and rest?'

'Well, I'll maybe sit in a chair in the living-room with this thing propped up for a couple of days,' he grumbled. And with a grin at Lindsey's severe air, 'All right, three or four days then.'

That was as near to getting him to promise to take things slowly for a while as they could manage.

Meanwhile, Lindsey stormed to herself over the two men's amicable relationship. It got crazier by the minute. Not only had Brance MacKenzie set up home for himself on Springlands property, he was now actually standing in for her father after calmly coming along and dictating to him abut their trees!

The sun was lowering in the sky when they arrived at Springlands. The house had a mellow air in the softened light. Indoors the dappled glow slanting through the windows gave a warmth to the rather rambling living-room.

Lindsey was conscious as she had never been before of the shabby décor. She was foolishly content to know that each item of furniture gleamed with polish, as did the wooden floor strewn with bright rugs.

Brance settled Ben into a comfortable armchair and Lindsey brought him a padded stool on which to rest his leg. She purposely disappeared then, and spent some time searching out a cover in her bedroom that she could drape around her father. Annoyingly, Brance was still there when she returned. He was strolling around the room, stopping before knick-knacks and framed photographs.

Lindsey spread the rug over her father, ignoring his protests. She tucked him in leisurely. But far from showing any signs of leaving, Brance had taken to musing over the various bowls of flowers dotted around, which were still fresh from when she had arranged them yesterday. 'Aracea, begonioceae, olea-ceae,' he said knowledgeably. And viewing the effect as a whole as she made to pass him by hintingly a second time, 'I see you're not just a forest harpy.'

She had just measured up a retort to this remark when a footstep sounded behind them. 'Good afternoon. I hope I'm not intruding?'

The man who had entered the room eyed Brance, whose grin in that instance was openly provoking, with cool curiosity and veiled resentment. He was almost as tall as the forestry man and around the same age, mid-thirties. He was dressed elegantly, if casually, in ice-blue slacks and tailored shirt. Some might have said that his smile was a little slick, but his features were handsome. In fact Lindsey hadn't noticed until this moment just how handsome. 'Nick!' she beamed. 'What a pleasant surprise!'

'I heard about Ben's accident.' He came forward. 'I thought I'd drop in to see how things were.'

'How good of you to come over and enquire.'

Gushingly, she ushered him in. 'Isn't that thoughtful of him, Dad, when he's so busy managing the sugar estates?'

Ben greeted the new arrival with dubious humour. 'Hello, Nick. As you can see, I can't get up to welcome you.'

It was he who introduced the two men. 'Nicholas Mollenda, our neighbour. Nick, meet Brance Mackenzie. He works for an organisation that's trying to prevent the despoliation of South American forests.'

'So I have heard.' Lindsey had the feeling that the two men were weighing each other up while they shook hands briefly. 'Luckily there are not many trees on Mollenda property—we specialise in cassava and sugar—so I suppose we escape the blade of your kind of intervention, Mr Mackenzie.'

'Contrary to popular supposition,' Brance said drily, 'we don't enjoy causing upsets in a forestry community.'

Ben was feeling expansive now that he was comfortably propped up. 'Well, Lindy, don't keep our guests hanging about. Sit down, boys. What shall we have to drink?'

'The doctor said no alcohol for a day or two,' Lindsey warned. 'You're to have something palliative, like tea.'

'Well, why don't we all have a cup of tea?' Brance suggested. Though Lindsey didn't meet his gaze, she detected a note of mockery in his tones. So he thought she had scant idea of the social graces!

'If Nick doesn't mind,' she purposely sought out their neighbour's approval, 'I'll go and prepare a tray.'

'That will be very nice,' he gave her a smile. 'I can't think of a more charming novelty than Lindsey serving tea for us all.'

She left the men to talk among themselves and went through the house to the kitchen. Zina, their help around the house, was preparing vegetables for the evening meal. Of African extraction, she was plump and pleasant-faced, and cooked and cleaned at Springlands for all but two days of the week when she went to Moratica to visit her married daughter and grandchildren.

She would have prepared the tea-tray herself, but Lindsey told her with some determination, 'It's all right, Zina. I'll see to the guests.'

She leafed out the prettiest tray-cover in the drawer for the base. Then she set out the flowered bone china which had been her mother's. If the cups were rather dainty for a man's hand, well this only filled her with a certain malicious satisfaction.

She made sandwiches of wafer-thin bread, cut them into postage-stamp size, and begged some of the tiny, iced, fancy cakes which Zina had baked for her grandchildren. She had an idea the Negress was eyeing her work with a startled wonder, bearing in mind the sound of male voices drifting from the living-room. This only served to boost her enjoyment.

She placed sufficient embroidered napkins on the edge of the tray and with over-stated grandeur transported the whole thing through.

Throughout the afternoon tea ritual, she gave her attention to Nick. Her father was too engrossed in the masculine company to notice much of what he ate and drank. Their neighbour was no doubt accustomed to such ornamentation in the gracious Mollenda household. But Brance . . . She hoped he was choking on the minute bites and finding it difficult to pick up his delicate tea-cup.

The Mollendas were proud of their Portuguese

heritage. It was said that there was a touch of the
Amerindian in their blood from a distant, indiscreet
relationship, though Nick never mentioned this. He was
wholly the Portuguese Don, supervising the running of
the family estate for his ageing father. But sometimes
Lindsey felt that something in his olive-skinned features
was faintly reminiscent of the Amerindians in the bush.

The conversation during the refreshments inevitably
centred around the men's work. Brance mentioned an
insecticide he had heard of against sugar-cane pest, for
Nick's benefit. Ben was keen to discuss anything
which would give him ideas for setting up something
other than logging on Springlands.

Lindsey bristled privately at his calm acceptance of
the situation thrust on them by the arrival of Brance
Mackenzie. She also noticed her father's growing
fatigue in the early evening light.

'It's time I was settling you in bed, Dad,' she said as
she rose. 'It was a long ride from town and you're not
exactly all in one piece.' As she expected, he put up no
great argument.

The men got to their feet in accordance with this
suggestion and prepared to leave. Over-politely Nick
said in Brance's direction, 'Can I give you a lift
somewhere?'

'Thanks, but I've got the logging truck outside.' He
cast a glance towards the armchair. 'So long, Ben. We'll
keep in touch. Thanks for the tea, Lindsey.'

'Don't mention it.' She dared him to mock her now,
yet his look matched hers for irony. He gave a brief nod
in Nick's direction and went out.

She made a point of strolling casually to the outdoors
with their neighbour. She idled beside his immaculate
estate car while Brance started up the rickety truck and
finally rumbled off.

'Lindsey,' Nick was immediately intense when they were alone, 'what on earth possesses your father to allow that man into his home? I can tell you, if he had come on to my land giving his orders I would have used a whip to demonstrate my distaste for snooping strangers.'

The disparaging way he referred to Brance irked her, but she wouldn't let herself be affected by it. 'Dad has this idea that he's only doing his job,' she shrugged.

'And does his job include indulging in intimate moments with the daughter of the man he has ruined?' he asked almost angrily. 'I saw the way he looked at you when I entered the room.'

Lindsey was a little bemused at his mood. She had known Nick since arriving at Springlands when she was seventeen. They were friends in a distant sort of way— she had her work and he had his. Neither, as far as she knew, had regarded the relationship as anything but platonic. And she had certainly never detected jealousy in Nick before.

'You needn't worry about Brance Mackenzie wearing down my opposition,' she said brusquely. 'He may have convinced my father that the termination of work in our southland stretch of forest is inevitable, but I'm far from amenable to the idea.'

'I'm glad to hear that, Lindsey.' While his smile was white and attractive, a tiny frown played across his brow as he added, 'I've heard that Mackenzie is working on your land on his own account.

'There's nothing I can do about that, I'm afraid.' She sighed to hide her mixed feelings on the matter. Of course she hated the idea of Brance making himself comfortable on their property. On the other hand she had grown used to having him around to fight with. 'Dad's still the boss of the Davis Logging Company,' she tacked on, to side-step the issue where she was concerned.

'Well, I don't like him wandering around those southern reserves unhampered,' Nick said harshly. 'What's he doing there anyway?'

Wondering why the fact that the forestry man had chosen to camp in their woods should upset Nick so much, she replied, 'He's taking samples of trees and flora, I think.'

'Then it'll be all the better for all of us when he packs up and moves on to annoy some other property owner.'

As though realising then that his manner was somewhat strained, his face cleared. With surprising tenderness he asked, 'Lindsey, how are you after all the troubles which have befallen your father? I really want to help, you know. I came over this afternoon to see if there was anything I could do for Ben while he's laid up.'

'You did!' Lindsey hoped she had successfully kept the startled note out of her voice. At the same time she had an idea. 'Well,' she said slowly while nursing a secret enjoyment, 'as you probably know, Dad went great guns in getting everything over to the new logging site. They spent a week or more setting up camp, now the whole thing has to be dismantled. Sam's a good man, but he doesn't have Dad's authority . . . and the lumberjacks are a little tetchy because there's no tree-sawing bonuses in the offing . . .'

'You mean you'd like me to go over there and exercise a little discipline over the men?'

'Something like that,' Lindsey murmured innocently. Well, she was heir to the Davis Logging Company wasn't she? Why shouldn't she have her say in who she would like to stand in for her father until he was on his feet again?

If Brance didn't care for her choice of temporary boss on the job he could always go back to gathering his posies!

# CHAPTER THREE

NICK left after assuring her that he would be at the logging site first thing in the morning. Lindsey went to get her father off to bed feeling considerably pleased with herself.

He didn't take kindly to being anchored to the armchair all the next day, but she was adamant. She spoiled him with his favourite meals, and played card games with him to pass the time. But by the following day they were both feeling the need for other diversions. 'There's no sense in the two of us going soft on the job,' he said when she had placed a pile of his much-loved logging magazines at his side. 'There ought to be one Davis finding out how things are going on the southlands site. Why don't you take the ranch-waggon, Lindy, and drive over there?'

She didn't want to admit that this thought had been on her mind most of the morning. And even if she *was* itching to get out there, it was Nick, she told herself, she was eager to see and confer with over the dismantling programme.

When she had instructed Zina to be on call for any of her father's requests, she drove away. Despite the ups and downs of the past week or more, she felt in reasonably good spirits. Her father's disability had now taken its place in their lives, and he was on the mend, thank heavens. Added to this comforting knowledge was the delicious freedom of the outdoors.

The Guyana countryside never failed to interest her. A huge tract of thick, hilly jungle and forest sloped down from this high plateau towards the sea. The belt running along the coast was devoted mainly to rice— for there was often flooding after the rains—and sugar.

Springlands property stretched for miles, sometimes overlapping on the jungle hillside. Tacana Hill was in this direction. One could see the bald area rising above the rain forests, and thinking of Brance, Lindsey averted her gaze a little guiltily. But, thankfully, they were re-planting after divesting the hill of its trees. She passed the Mollenda sugar estates, fields and fields of tall, swaying green and aimed for the forests.

As soon as the leafy canopy closed in overhead, the atmosphere changed. The blue sky and scudding clouds were shut out and a sombre silence, broken only by the screams of monkeys and bright-plumed birds, prevailed. She followed the river, straddled by the trees, to Danny Capucho's trading store.

Danny did business with traffic passing by on the dirt road to the town of Caibo in the south, and with the villages locally. But his fellow Amerindians were drifting more and more towards civilisation. Their tribal habits were breaking down, and the sense of community imposed by a primitive life was gradually disappearing.

She had a cool drink, made from a native plant, with Danny, passed the time of day with him, then pushed on up river.

When she arrived at the logging site, much of the machinery and trappings had disappeared. She left the ranch-waggon at the edge of the clearing. Sam came to meet her. To say that the work appeared to have gone with a swing, he didn't look in too happy a frame of mind.

'Some of the "jacks" have walked out. Packed up their personal belongings and took off.' Sam, never one to mince words, greeted her.

'You mean they've abandoned their jobs with the Davis Company?' Lindsey blinked.

'What can you expect with that Mollenda guy strutting round with his whip under his arm?' Sam spat out a disc of tobacco juice as a way of expressing his opinion.

'I'm sure he only sported it for effect,' she said, colouring slightly.

'Well, anyway, the men said they were not his sugar coolies slicing cane on his estate and they quit.'

'How many?'

'Six or seven.'

'Well,' she shrugged philosophically, 'there's going to be less work around shortly, so maybe it's for the best.'

Sam went off, muttering to himself, and Lindsey moved authoritatively among the rest of the men who were engaged in mopping-up operations.

She was having second thoughts now about the practicability of her mode of attire. Before leaving the house she had been smitten with a desire to present a slightly different picture to her usual khaki-clad appearance. But as it was still rough country where she was going, she had settled for a pair of frayed-edged jean shorts and a white shirt.

Now she realised she lacked the weight she was seeking as the boss's daughter in her present outfit. In fact some of the lumberjacks were blatantly insolent with their smiles as she passed them.

She came upon Brance half under the bulk of a camp generator which he and a handful of men were working to get into the back of a truck. 'If you're looking for Mollenda,' he said between breaths, 'he's taking the air near the river.' Because of the tremendous exertion imposed upon him, his features registered only effort, but there was no mistaking the satire in his voice.

Lindsey responded with a pondering look. 'I can't think why,' she cooed, 'you don't use the logging winch or one of the portable cranes to lift that thing up.'

'Your friend tidily got rid of all the hoisting equipment,' came the bland reply.

Lindsey hurried off. One couldn't blame Nick. He was, after all, a little above the rough and ready ways of a logging camp.

She found him tossing bits of palm kernel to a scarlet macaw on the river bank. He was faultlessly dressed in fawn riding breeches and tailored sports top. Though they were into the last hours of a working day, there wasn't a speck of logging site dust on him.

His face brightened when he saw her. He threw the bits of kernel carelessly into the water regardless of the macaw's avid interest and came towards her. 'Well,' he took her hands in his, 'are you pleased to see everything almost finished here, as I promised?'

'It's wonderful,' she smiled. 'The men must have worked hard to move all that equipment in a couple of days.'

'They were a little slow to fall in with my ideas.' There was humour in his hauteur. 'They do not have the training of my field hands, but we finally came to an understanding.'

Lindsey felt a little uncomfortable when she thought of Sam's comments about the whip, but surely it was the end result that counted?

Nick strolled with her through the trees. It seemed natural now that his arm should turn about her waist. 'I love these forests, don't you?' she sighed gazing about her with mixed feelings. 'It's a pity that trees are useful for so many things in the world and that their wood normally fetches a good price on the market.'

'These will fetch no price at all as they are not now to

be cut,' he commented, adding with unexpected sympathy in his voice, 'what are you going to do, Lindsey, when the last of your father's timber reserves are exhausted? It must be a colossal worry for Ben.'

'He has known about the dwindling timber for some time,' she disclosed. 'He went to Georgetown to try and secure a loan to expand the saw-mill for leasing purposes, but it didn't come off.'

'I know. But he should have come to me. As your immediate neighbour and a good friend of the family—I hope—I should have been only too happy to discuss ways and means of helping him through a bad time.'

Nick knew that Dad had been seeking a loan! This news took Lindsay a little by surprise. She had thought it had been a well-kept secret between the two of them.

'You know us Davises,' she said lightly. 'We're independent to the last.'

'Not always a good thing,' he remarked sternly. 'And—I have to say this, Lindsey—I would have a lot more respect for your father as a logging man if he sent that forestry official Mackenzie packing, instead of allowing him to wander loose wherever he chooses around here.'

'That's Dad,' she shrugged. 'He believes in being fair no matter how much he's been bludgeoned in his business.'

Nick said then, with uncharacteristic magnanimity, 'Not being a timber man myself, I agree in part that our forests should be preserved where possible. But I certainly would not, under any circumstances, permit the man enforcing these kind of rules to linger, let alone camp, on my property.'

Lindsey half-smiled to herself as they walked. Poor Nick! He did seem rather put out at Brance's presence in these parts. Still, it was refreshing to know she had an ally. After all, these were her feelings exactly, weren't they?

She had thought that he would drop his arm from about her waist when they came out into the clearing. Oddly enough, he kept it there until they had covered the distance to where Brance was now slotting a rope through the unstable objects on the truck.

'I see you managed the generator without too much trouble,' he observed with satisfaction. 'A simple question of brawn co-ordination, as I pointed out.'

'The next time you're let loose around a logging camp dismantling,' Brance continued working with the rope, 'remember to leave the hauling gear till last. Unless you're employing a herd of bull elephants to get the stuff into the trucks.'

'In many cases animals are a better choice than man for performing one's labours,' Nick said suavely.

'You mean they don't offer the same kind of protest when they're pushed to the limit,' Brance smiled over the knot he was tying.

'We all have our own ways of getting the job done. I personally don't look for popularity, only results. And Lindsey appears to be well pleased with my efforts.'

'For a guy who's not fishing for compliments, you do all right, Mollenda.'

To the snide look Brance cast her way, Lindsey replied, 'As a matter of fact I think Nick is to be admired, coming here at my request when he knows nothing at all about a lumberjack's work, to help us get all this stuff transferred back to the base camp.'

'I guess I've used up all my admiration for the day on the men who got this lot into the trucks,' Brance said drily.

'I'm pleased to see they're not wasting their time in light exercises like tying ropes.' Nick strove for verbal superiority.

If this was meant to flick Brance on the raw it came to nothing. He simply smiled and said, 'Loyalty's a funny thing. It can make some men walk away from a good boss in disgust. What's left of them around here have enough going for Ben to know where the work is.'

Nick was not a man to show discomfort. He did, however, demonstrate a desire to be off. 'Having conformed to the wishes of a fair lady in distress,' he said almost gaily, 'I shall now have the reward of driving the said fair lady home. Are you ready, Lindsey?'

She gave him a lopsided smile. 'Unfortunately I've got the ranch-waggon. I'll have to drive it back, I'm afraid.' Then on an inspiration, for Brance's benefit, 'But I can follow behind you all the way, if you like.'

'I suppose I will have to be content with that.' His grin was attractive as he spread an arm for her to join him in their walk to the cars. But before she had reached his side he said, 'By the way, the hotel in town is giving a dance on Saturday night. I would consider it fair payment for my attempts as a logging man if you would accompany me for the evening.'

Lindsey was slightly taken aback by this suggestion, though naturally she didn't let it show. She knew that Nick's tastes in entertainment usually ran to something more expensive than the Moratica social gathering. She had heard that when he wanted a break from the sugar estates, he spent his time frequenting the race course or playing golf in Georgetown. But of course now she gushed, 'How very sweet of you, Nick. Far from repaying a debt, I can assure you I would be delighted.'

'It's a date, then. I'll call for you at six.' Not only did he escort her to the ranch-waggon, but he carefully assisted her inside.

His own car was parked some way off, at the edge of

the main track. She waited to give him time to clear the first belt of trees then, flamboyantly and with a great deal of show, she started up and drove off.

She had reached the track and was moving in readiness for following in the wake of the fast-receding estate car when into her vision at the side came the loaded logging truck. Travelling at right angles, it appeared to be crazily making for the river, or in the act of wrapping itself round one of the giant greenhearts. Mercifully it did neither, but came to rest smack across the track only yards ahead of her, where its front wheels sank up to the axles in a patch of riverside mud.

Her way well and truly blocked, Lindsey flung out of the ranch-waggon and marched over. Brance was just leaving the truck cab. 'Funny,' he scratched his head, 'I could have sworn I gauged it just right for taking off along the track.'

Not fooled, Lindsey fumed, 'You did that on purpose! You deliberately drove that heap across my path so that I wouldn't be able to follow Nick as we planned!'

'Now why should I want to do a thing like that?' Leisurely, Brance pondered over the mud-bound wheels.

'Jealousy perhaps,' she said airily. The look he gave her demolished much of this high-flown theory. She was reduced to asking, 'Why don't you like Nick?'

His tones were mockingly incredulous. 'Who says I don't like him?'

'You were unpleasant, almost rude to him just now.'

'Well, you make up for my lack of fancy manners where he's concerned.' Brance set about getting the truck out of the mud.

She watched him root out sacking and oddments from the tool box and said, 'I've known Nick for five years. Ever since I first came to Guyana.'

'And it's taken him all this time to invite you to the local hop?'

Her cheeks warmed slightly at this, but she recovered her equilibrium to remark, 'Perhaps he's feeling the competiton.'

'A guy who only moves when competition's around might turn out a bit lumpish in the long term.'

'I can't imagine anyone less lumpish than Nick,' she said dreamily. 'He's tall, charming——'

'And calculating.'

Shaken from her pose, she shot the khaki-clad figure a glance. 'He's wealthy, and makes an excellent job of running the sugar estates. Why should he need to be calculating?' she asked.

'I don't know. Just a hunch I have. I found him sifting through the soil at the back of the camp yesterday.'

This caused Lindsey to ponder slightly, but she wasn't long in finding an answer. 'Well, it's like Nick to want to help out,' she said. 'He was probably checking to see if any of our open land hereabouts can be made to produce crops of some kind. Poor soil has defeated many a venture in Guyana over the centuries, as the old, derelict sugar plantations show.'

'Maybe you're right,' Brance drawled. The lack of conviction in his tones riled her afresh.

'You're intent on seeing the worst in Nick, aren't you?' she snapped. 'I haven't noticed you giving any thanks for his help in clearing the site.'

The smile he gave her was loaded with something unpleasant. 'You'll have heard,' he placed the sacking round the wheels, 'that you've got a considerably reduced work-force due to his Latin arrogance.

'Latin arrogance, Scottish-cum-Canadian arrogance. I don't see there's much difference.'

If she had known that he was due to pass her so close on his way to the back of the truck, she might not have been so flaunting with her reply. Too late, she felt his fingers clamp around her wrist and roughly, he jerked her against him. 'The difference is,' that unpleasant smile still played about his lips, 'I reserve mine for keeping logging bosses' daughters from getting too big for their frilly pants. And the next time I see you walking among your men dressed like this I'll personally cart you off and put a pair of my own forestry drills on those damnably provocative legs of yours.'

So he found her legs provocative, at least! The satisfaction of this, coupled with the ache of excitement coursing through her at his touch, caused her almost to lose her fiery mood of resentment. 'You can't tell me what to do,' she flashed, the curved of her body heaving against him.

'I shouldn't have to. I'd like to bet Ben doesn't agree with your wandering round his timber camps half-naked.'

'You love to exaggerate, don't you?' His 'frilly pants' comment had reminded her uncomfortably of his familiarity with her more intimate garments. Added to that, was the discomfort of knowing that her father would not approve of her present outfit in the work area.

She hotly skirted the tiresome subject. 'Nick didn't have any stuffy ideas on my mode of dress. Or if he did, he was too polite to mention it. But you wouldn't notice that. You were too intent on fanning the antagonism between the two of you.'

'If you think we were circling each other like a pair of randy stags over you, forget it.' He thrust her away from him and reached in for planks from the back of the truck.

Her feminine ego was badly mauled by this comment. There was nothing more exhilarating to a woman, she had been telling herself for some time, than to have two men at hostile variance on her account.

Now she watched Brance, going about his work, in a mildly deflated way. It had not been her imagination, she was certain, that the two men had disliked each other on sight. But now she was not so sure why. She was reasonably certain that she figured somewhere in their enmity, but there was something else. Something which brought to mind the figure of the tall, raven-haired Guyanese, of Portuguese extraction, with saturnine good looks and an inherent hauteur.

Was it Nick? she asked herself. Was he the kind of man who fostered an instinctive wariness in his fellow males? He was pleasant and well-groomed, but he did not, as far as she knew, have any close friends among his own sex.

Everything ready to try out, Brance climbed into the cab of the truck and switched on the engine. Lindsey stood by, waiting with undisguised pleasure for all his efforts to come to nothing. Much to her disgust the vehicle climbed out of the ditch at the first try. It was skilfully manoeuvred until it came to rest on the dry track.

'Good. Now we can get going.' She slid behind the wheel of the ranch-waggon, itching to be off. If she burnt up the route a bit she still might catch Nick up.

That was her plan, but she didn't get a chance to put it into practice. Brance, rumbling idly along in the truck up ahead, hogged the centre of the track along the whole of the forest route.

Lindsey was very much at a loose end over the next few days. She played armchair games with her father, fiddled about the garden, washed her hair and tried unsuccessfully to read a book.

She wouldn't admit to a longing to see Brance again, if only to fight. And even if she did, there was not one stick of equipment left on the site near his cabin that she could make the excuse of going to collect.

Far from missing him, she told herself fumingly, she was more interested in spiking his obvious contentment at being allowed to potter around as he liked on *their* property. But Brance was not a man that one could easily get the better of.

To offset her frustrations in this direction, she visited the Tacana lumber camp in the capacity of the boss's daughter. On behalf of her father she observed the felling, bucking—which was cross-cutting into logs— and limbing of the timber. She toured the area where the mechanical debarker was in action, and watched the skidding of logs by tractors using steel cables.

Unexpectedly, when she returned home to Springlands to report on excellent progress at the Tacana site, her father was not in too pleased a mood.

With the help of a crutch, he had now gravitated to his study in the afternoons. It was a book-lined, sparsely furnished room which he also used as his work office. On the road coming in she had passed a logger in a runabout. She discovered now that he had delivered the latest labour sheets to the house.

'Look at this,' Ben tapped the papers broodingly. 'Seven of my best men. Gone. Packed it in.'

'Shows what a good boss you are,' Lindsey commented a little uncomfortably. 'When you're not on the job, dissatisfaction is rife.'

'Some of those loggers have been with me for years,' he was puzzled and angry. 'I'd like to know what Mackenzie was playing at. He must have rubbed them one hell of the wrong way for a walk-out like that.'

Lindsey lowered her lashes, curtailing the smile that wanted to steal around her lips. Maybe she had found a way to turf Brance out of his cosy cabin. 'Well, let's face it,' she shrugged, 'he's only a forestry man. He spends his time studying plant life and tree diseases. What can he know about our men and the way they work?'

'I was willing to stake my life that he was a level-headed type.' Ben shook his head disbelievingly. 'He's got a pretty important job and he won't have got there strewing scalps all the way.'

'Well, he appears to have strewn some of ours,' Lindsey said carefully. 'I suppose you'll be thinking twice now about letting him do as he pleases on our land?'

'You're darned right I will.'

Ben glowered over the labour sheets and Lindsey went off to take a shower. While she was under the jets of water, she soaped herself with feline satisfaction. Who said Brance Mackenzie was all-powerful around here?

After drifting at a loose end most of Saturday, Lindsey decided to take special care over her preparations for the dance, for Nick's sake. She had an anxious moment when she thought of leaving her father all alone in the house. She had been so busy accepting Nick's invitation loudly within Brance's range of hearing, she had forgotten that Zina always spent the weekends with her family.

'I've got a date in town tonight,' she disclosed in the living-room, 'but I'm not sure I should go off and leave you all on your own.'

'I'm neither senile nor does this plaster-cast con-
traption stop me from getting round the house any less
agilely than you do.' Ben shot her an indignant look
which subsided into one of sly but eager enquiry. 'A
date? Who with?'

'Nick has invited me to the hotel dance.' She made
the announcement importantly and felt rather deflated
when her father returned to his newspaper and said
absently, 'Oh, Nick.'

A flicker of irritation moved her to remark, 'I
thought you liked Nick.'

'I do. He and I have always got on okay together,
but . . .'

'But what?' she almost snapped. Then bridging the
silence in exasperation, 'Don't tell me you're getting a
soft spot for that odious forestry man, after all he's
done to us?'

She had taken care to stress her meaning and after a
moment, as though recalling those labour-sheet reports,
Ben nodded, 'You're right. Have a good time, Lindy.
Nick's a good sort.'

Lindsey left the room in mixed mood. She would
have felt happier if there had been a little more
conviction in his voice.

To show that she herself considered Nick far more
acceptable in the Davis household than Brance
Mackenzie, she made a special effort to look her best
for the dance.

At six o'clock she kissed her father on the cheek and
went out to the waiting shooting-brake. She thought
she was looking rather stunning in blue silk dress,
dainty shoes and her hair loose and waving on her
shoulders. But after a brief smile of approval, Nick
went round to the driving seat and they were off on the
road to town.

She had imagined them chatting about this and that on the long drive. Instead he switched on the radio. At least the music was soft and dreamy. She found she rather liked sitting beside Nick and bowling along in the gathering dusk. He was looking darkly attractive in a tailored evening suit with a sheen to it.

It was almost seven-thirty when they arrived at the hotel. Things were just beginning to liven up. Every once in a while the town authorities arranged a get-together for the outlying mining and timberwood communities and townspeople alike. It usually took the form of loaded buffet tables in the hotel dining-room and a group of musicians imported from Georgetown playing in the only space big enough in Moratica for such an occasion, the adjoining conference hall. This was a rather grand name for a wooden building where the price of sugar cane and other estate produce was bandied over from time to time.

Lindsey had been to more than one of these Saturday night affairs with her father, but tonight was different. Tonight she was on the arm of Nick.

Disappointingly, he met a couple of sugar-estate owners at the buffet tables and she was more or less obliged to help herself to the snacks provided and amuse herself watching the other occupants of the room.

There were no varying social stratas in Moratica. The Arawak and Carib Amerindians employed in the cattle and logging industries rubbed shoulders with independent farmers and landowners and the European element. The women were a mixture of dark-skinned, neatly dressed Guyanese and sloe-eyed beauties from over the borders of Venezuela and Brazil.

At last the men split up and, business forgotten, Nick was by her side. He made her feel very special, choosing

what he thought she would most enjoy from the buffet
tables. Unfortunately she had already filled herself up
with food for the sake of something to do, but she
nibbled happily while they stood close together amid
the throng.

Secretly she felt rather important in Nick's company.
He had an expensive, polished air which set him apart
from the other men in the room. If he appeared to be
set apart too from the hearty handshakes going on
about her, she didn't let herself notice.

When they had finished at the buffet tables he said
unexpectedly, turning an arm about her waist, 'Shall we
dance, or would you like to go for a walk in the
garden?'

With a little laugh she shrugged, 'A breath of air
might be nice first. It is a little crowded in here.'

As gardens went, the paths they strolled a few
minutes later were hardly the conventional type. The
feather-headed crowns of coconut palms dusted the
starlit sky. At eye-level tufted grasses and crabwood
battled with flowering shrubs for prominence.

Nick held her hand and for a while they walked in
silence. Or comparative silence, for there was much
whooping and jollity coming from the region of the
hotel interior. Lindsey thought it was only natural that
the men should want to let off a little steam after a long
period of back-breaking toil in the interior, but Nick
confirmed his apparent distaste for the ribaldry by
remarking, 'Give a worker a few Guyana dollars in his
pocket and leave to come to town, and he turns into a
buffoon.'

'I suppose it's the feeling of freedom they get away
from the job,' Lindsey smiled. 'Camp life can be pretty
restricting and a lot of these men have their wives and
families in other countries.'

'Too much freedom has never been a good thing for a worker.' Nick's features appeared sharp and saturnine in the shadows. 'They get careless after a binge and it's usually us property owners who have to suffer the result of their neglect.'

Lindsey found her smile becoming fixed. Her father employed a considerable work-force. He allowed his men plenty of time off and they had never had to suffer shoddy workmanship as a result. Her mouth was forming into putting this point of view into words when Nick promptly lowered his head and covered her lips with his.

Taken completely unawares, she was not sure how to react. But after a while, she decided that the experience was not unpleasant. She leaned against him, his arms turned about her and for some time they remained locked against each other in this way.

When at last she was able to draw away she laughed a little breathlessly. 'Well! Do you always get your victims on the defensive before slaying them with that kind of argument!'

'I'm not in the habit of making amorous advances to attractive young women, but it's an idea.' He laughed too, briefly, and Lindsey had the feeling that he hadn't given the timing of the kiss much thought.

Because he had shown himself to be anything but a demonstrative man she was startled when he repeated the process a few seconds later, and when he suggested then that they go in and dance, she agreed in a kind of bemused state.

Some time later, mingling with the other couples on the floor, Lindsey found moving in Nick's arms a novel experience. Though he held her close and the occasional word of intimate chat passed between them, she sensed a remoteness in his manner. There were some people one never really got to know in this life, no matter how personal the relationship. It occurred to her as they danced that Nick was one such man. There was something locked away in his personality, a side to his nature that was fathomless to all but himself.

To make up for this he was attractive, charming and of commanding appearance. It was odd that he was all these things, yet—or was it her imagination that wherever they moved in the crowded interior his presence engendered a faintly hostile air?

There were many people Lindsey knew in Moratica. She hadn't lived for five years at Springlands without making the acquaintance of the usual tradespeople and so forth. To offset the mildly isolated feeling she was experiencing she cast a glance around with a view to acknowledging a friendly nod here and there. It was then that she spotted Brance at the far side of the hall amid a mixed group.

The sight of him started up all those odd, annoying workings of her body. Her pulses were fired into life against her will, her breathing became erratic, and little hammers of pleasure pounded at her temples just to know he was in the same room. In sheer disgust, she realised that her body had been hoping all along that he would show up tonight. Her heart and mind too, why deny it? But only—only, she told herself, so that she could preen in Nick's company.

She went out of her way to catch his eye as they danced by. He was dressed in a lightweight blue suit. Lean, weathered and insufferably relaxed, his attention was all for the attractive women in his group.

She was glad that the music, chiefly of a South-American flavour, had only just struck up for the present dance number. There would be lots more opportunities to flaunt in passing by his area. She wanted to flaunt her feminine allure, to show him that not all men brought out the tree shrew in her.

She devoted herself to dancing cleverly with Nick. In a keyed-up, breathless way, she had visions of him turning at a polite tap on the shoulder and finding herself in Brance's arms. Before entering this section of the building she had repaired her make-up in what served as a powder room and combed her hair till it fell soft and shining on her shoulders. And she knew that her dress was smart and flattering to her figure. It was infuriating to have gone to all this trouble—she might as well face it, she had only spent all those hours before the mirror at home in the hope of running into Brance—not to rate so much as a glance from that maddening, egotistical forestry man across the room.

As the evening wore on she stopped fishing for attention, albeit in a covert way, and became curious instead. Feminine conquests were probably legion in his life. He had said that he had been around and, judging by the way he was operating now, she didn't doubt it. Considering he had only just become acquainted with the sloe-eyed creature he was talking to, the conversation between them was deep and aggravatingly intimate.

When they weren't dancing, Nick chattered in his aloof way with fellow sugar-cane growers and cattle owners. Rustic types themselves, with plump, gaily-dressed wives, they appeared a little surprised to see him at the gathering, confirming Lindsey's own theory that he normally preferred the more sophisticated pastimes of Georgetown.

The night air in Guyana is noted for its high humidity content. As the interior grew progressively stickier, Nick suggested that they go for a drink. There was a spacious bar area at the far end of the hall. Doors were open to the night and some of the chairs at the circular tables were occupied.

It wasn't until she and Nick were standing beside the bar, drinks in hand, that she noticed the familiar faces of the group sat at the table immediately to the side of them. These were her father's men ... or had been. She realised with a feathering of apprehension that the bunch, who were rather the worse for drink and inclined to be bawdy, were the lumberjacks who had walked off the job recently on the southland site.

As she had feared they wasted no time raising their voices in a ribald, embittered way when their bleary gazes focused on Nick at the bar. 'Well look who's dropped in to add a touch of class to the proceedings,' Ray Araka, a beefy individual was eloquent in his distaste. 'None other than our whip-toting pansy boy, the sugar king himself.'

'Where do you reckon he gets all those fancy clothes?' another one slurred. 'It must be his whippy hand that brings in them dollars, he sure as hell don't soil his dainty fingers in the cane fields.'

A dark flush spread beneath the surface of Nick's saturnine features. Lindsey thought he would have suggested that they move somewhere else. It must have been his Portuguese pride which kept him anchored to the bar, exuding an air of being totally oblivious to the jibes.

She was a little hurt that the lumberjacks, who had always had a friendly word for her around her father's logging camps, now went out of their way to ignore her presence. At least all but one of them. When big Ray came up to order more drinks he cast her a slack grin. ' 'Evening, Miss Davis. Slumming tonight, ain't yer? There's some mighty fine specimens of bush rat in the locale if you want to improve on present company.'

Sipping her drink, she lowered her lashes over the heat in her cheeks. When she raised them, Ray was thankfully just departing with a cluster of beer glasses in each beefy fist. In passing he flicked a wrist with a wink at his mates, then raised his eyebrows in mock concern as a river of the pungent smelling brew trickled down Nick's immaculate front. 'Well now! Wasn't that clumsy of me! And too bad I just don't happen to have a thing on me to mop up the frilly shirt front.'

There was a roar of appreciative laughter from the table. It was a combination of this, his soaked person, and the logging man's leering defiance which snapped Nick's self-control.

'You *scum*!' His tones of withering disdain seemed to wash like ice particles over the animation at the other tables. A hush settled over the area. All eyes turned towards the bar.

Lindsey sensed several of the male occupants of the room tensing for action. She prayed that the thing was not going to develop into a brawl. She was wondering how they could extricate themselves from a mood which Nick's haughty contempt only incensed, when a voice spoke up from the far end of the bar.

'Hey, Ray! You getting jittery in your drinking ways because you're out of a job?' Brance strolled smilingly on to the scene. He cast a glance over Nick's stained suit and added, 'I guess Mr Mollenda will overlook your shaky beer hand this time.' Then clapping an arm round the burly shoulders, 'The thing is, there's no need for you guys to be drowning your sorrows in these parts. I was over at Tacana Hill yesterday. They're crying out for your help with those wallaba giants.'

'Is that a fact?' Big Ray blinked as he was led away.

'Right. And there's a nice fat bonus for anyone who reports back to the camp for work.'

'You hear that, boys?' Ray joined in the scrabble for personal gear at the table. 'Come on, let's get going!'

With the men's departure talk returned to normal at the other tables. Nick frowned at his stained appearance and abruptly excused himself. Almost before he was out of sight, Brance guided Lindsey forcefully towards the nearest doorway. He didn't need to hustle. She was only too eager to go somewhere private where she could let him know what she thought of his brainy ideas.

'You're good at coming up with solutions at someone else's expense, aren't you?' she carped furiously once they were out under the stars. 'Where do you think we're going to find fat bonuses for seven men when the Davis Company is on the point of ruin, thanks to you?'

'As you're supposedly in command while your father's indisposed, you work it out,' he said simply.

Oh, she wanted to wipe that grin off his face! Not because of his reply, but because every part of her rejoiced because he had stepped into her life again. Her heart was a slave to every nuance of expression in his crinkled eyes. Her whole being was alive and reverberating at the mere contemplation of his touch.

And how she hated herself for these traitorous feelings. How could one fall hopelessly and blindly in love with a man whose mere appearance on the scene had brought chaos and unhappiness into their lives? One didn't. At least Lindsey Davis didn't. She considered she owed it to her father, no matter what his opinions were on the subject, to rid themselves of Brance Mackenzie at the earliest possible moment.

'I'd like to think I was in command,' she flared anew because of a yearning to be in his arms, 'but some self-opinionated type around here keeps trying to get in on the act.'

'Don't tell me you weren't glad to see me just now?'

At his mocking smile, she averted her glance. That was just it. She would always be pathetically glad to see Brance. And his intervention in the ugly scene of a few moments ago couldn't have been carried off with more tact or diplomacy. Hang it! Why did he have to be so ... so admirably cool?

'I'm sure Nick would have known what to do.' She tried not to let her reply sound lame.

'I didn't notice him doing over-much to protect you from an unpleasant scene,' Brance drawled. 'Seemed to me he was more wrapped up in the discomfort of having beer chucked over him.'

'Why is everyone so unfair about Nick?' she snapped. 'Just because he has rather more breeding than most people in these parts and prefers to dress elegantly, everyone has a down on him. Of course it's just jealousy. His kind always attract it.'

'Sure, that's what it is,' Brance said drily. 'But what puzzles me,' he added thoughtfully, 'is what is he doing here in town? From what I've heard his life-style usually centres around his sugar estates and the more sophisticated pursuits at the coast.'

'We did have a date,' Lindsey threw back her head proudly. 'And Nick being the considerate type, he probably realised I wouldn't want to leave Dad to go all the way to the capital, so like the gentleman he is, he chose the local dance for our evening out.'

'Could be,' Brance rubbed his chin. 'But knowing he'd be like a fish out of water here, why didn't he wait until he could take you to Georgetown? Why the hurry?'

'I don't exactly have two heads,' she preened sarcastically, 'and I do have most of the normal attributes of a woman. Maybe Nick finds me attractive.'

'Could be that he's just woken up to the fact after all these years that he's got a neatly packaged, honey-maned spitfire on his doorstep . . . whereas I,' he pulled her against him, 'recognised your womanly charms at first glance—there should be a moral there some-where . . .'

'Are you sure *moral* is the right word?' She arched her eyebrow rather than arch her back to drink in his nearness through every particle of her being.

'Well, if it was immoral of me to appreciate what I saw curled up beside my camp fire that night, I guess I'm the world's worst sinner.'

His eyes had a peculiar light in them, and she knew as sure as she felt her blood coursing through her like liquid fire that his mouth was about to descend on hers. Though withdrawal from the thought of sweet surrender was agonising, she avoided his lips and said coldly, 'Considering I came here with another man your audacity knows no bounds, does it?'

'I thought you liked the competition.' There were sparks in his glance now. 'For instance, how does this compare with Mollenda's style of lovemaking in the garden earlier?'

So he had seen her go outdoors with Nick at the beginning of the evening!

Lindsey had no time to dwell on this flash of thought for every treacherous fibre in her was busy rejoicing in his forceful embrace. But there was no pain mingling with the overriding sweetness, of knowing his mouth on hers.

Perhaps her cool rejection had goaded him into being brutal. Her spine felt as though it would snap in two in his ruthless hold on her, in this kind of wild rapture. She surfaced dragging her bruised lips away from his with a little cry, and said between angry breaths, 'As I mentioned, Nick is a gentleman.'

'Don't tell me he didn't stir you right down to your toe ends with those swarthy good looks of his?'

Lindsey concentrated on trying to break free from his suffocating embrace. She didn't want to have to disclose that she found Nick remarkably cold compared to the forestry man's vibrant personality.

'No?' As though he guessed, he proceeded to practice his own brand of nerve-tingling techniques until, weak and spent against him, his lips travelling along her throat and brushing her ears, she begged, 'Brance, will you stop demonstrating that you're not all tree man and take me inside?'

'Sure thing,' he joked, though his voice was hoarse. 'Why don't we go to the bar and have a nice aspirin-laced lemonade each?'

When they had been served with something a little stronger than lemonade, Lindsey said sourly, 'I'm surprised you aren't itching to get back to your lady friends. Such popularity must be wearing at times.'

'I take it all in my stride,' he shrugged with aggravating self-assurance.

When Nick returned, the hotel staff had done a passable job sponging and pressing his jacket and shirt. But as she expected, he had only one thought in mind after the distasteful incident—to quit the premises. After a curt nod in Brance's direction, he escorted her away and out to his car.

Lindsey really had no objections. It would be late when they arrived home anyway. And, still shaking after that hatefully pleasurable session under the stars, she was more than eager to put as much distance as possible between herself and Brance.

# CHAPTER FOUR

BY the time they reached Springlands she was passably relaxed. Nick was not a talker and the evening had left a lot to be desired in both their minds. They had traversed the night miles of open grasslands, savannah and forest stretches, with little to say to each other. That was why, to Lindsey, it was somewhat unexpected when he showed a desire to linger on the drive.

The house was all in darkness save for the porch light. Her father would have gone to bed ages ago. Nick opened the car doors while they sat contemplating the night. The air was warm and throbbing with insect life. His face, which had been set for most of the drive, was now softened by a handsome smile. 'Whenever I hear a tinamou,' he said, as though the evening couldn't have gone smoother, 'I always think of a visit I made to our ancestral home in Brazil years ago. The birds had nested in the ruins. They fly badly, but they're excellent runners, and the men I'd hired to round them up earned their wages removing them bodily.'

Lindsey smiled at the throaty gurgle of the fowl-like creatures who were active at night and asked, 'Were there Mollendas in Brazil?'

'For a time,' he nodded. 'My grandfather told me that when there was rain there was goats' milk, cheese and beef and beans. But in the years of drought, when the hot winds blew from Africa, the effects were appalling.'

'Is there nothing left of the old life there now?' She was trying to picture an old plantation mansion such as that on the adjoining sugar estate.

'It was cotton and cacao in those days. The family estates have long since disappeared.' He added off-handedly, 'I bought some land in the area while I was there. I may go back one day and put the Mollendas back on the map again.'

The tinamous forgotten then, he drew her against him. The rather odd topic of conversation for a lovely starlit night, together with his abrupt way of placing his lips on hers, told Lindsey that he was a man who felt awkward at lovemaking. Desperate herself to push Brance's image from her mind, she did all she could to hide the fact that she found him a stilted lover. This was what she needed, she told herself. Someone else's arms about her. Someone else's masculine nearness stirring her senses. Someone to make her forget that a man like Brance had ever existed. And why not Nick?

He was obviously of the same mind. He rasied his head to say softly, 'This has been a memorable evening for us both, Lindsey. We have, I feel, a common bond against outsiders, and perhaps we have wasted too much time in the past behaving simply as neighbours.'

As she wasn't quite sure what to reply to this she lay, heart thudding, against him. After a moment, he murmured, 'May I take it that the years we have known one another are sufficient basis for me to regard you as someone very special in my life?'

'Of course, Nick,' she lifted her lips to his in smiling acquiescence.

After a few moments he seemed conscious of the late hour. She left the car and he raised a hand as he drove off. 'Good night, Lindsey. I'll be in touch.'

She strolled towards the porch in a reasonably contented frame of mind. What a strange evening it had been! But it had ended well. Nick was fond of her. With him she could forget that there had ever been any upset at Springlands. And there was something else that made quite pleasurable musing, despite the lumberjacks' incident tonight. Her smile curved maliciously as she tiptoed indoors.

Her father wouldn't know about the men's return to work for several days. He was hopping mad about their walk-out, apparently because of the forestry man's bad management. She was going to enjoy every minute of knowing that Brance Mackenzie had been told to get off their land.

Tidying the living-room the next morning, Lindsey smiled tolerantly to herself at the mess. Judging by the extra drinking glass, empty beer bottles and tobacco packets lying around, her father had had company last night.

She didn't give this discovery much thought until later when Ben was up and about. His countenance was not its usual rosy self and she soon found out why.

'You didn't tell me that Nick was over at the southland site when we were quitting the spot,' he said accusingly.

'That's right. He offered his help and so I accepted. I thought you'd welcome the extra pair of hands as you couldn't get over there yourself.' She made an effort to sound off-hand.

'I think we can do without that kind of help,' Ben replied drily. 'A wholesale walk-out has never been known in the fifteen years I've run this outfit.'

'That's what comes of having temporary bosses, I suppose,' she shrugged. 'I mean, Brance Mackenzie is the one who oozes authority around here, and he's the reason we were having to pack up and leave anyway. It's most likely his presence which upset the men into——'

'Lindy. Sam was here last night. He told me the whole story.'

She bit her lip, shot a look across the room and blustered, 'And I suppose your old buddy twisted it all in the forestry man's favour. Honestly, you'd think that ... that tree doctor was Santa Claus around here, instead of ruination to the Davis Logging Company.'

Ben smiled then. It was the tender, tolerant smile of a father for his daughter. 'You're young, Lindy,' he said. 'When you get to my and Sam's stage in life you learn to bend with the wind. There's no point in hurling yourself against it.'

'Well, you do it your way and I'll do it mine. As you've said, one day it will all belong to me, and I intend to see that we're running a thriving logging business despite the Mackenzie types in this world.'

She left the room then on the pretext of work elsewhere. Maybe her father and Sam had mellowed to the point where fight didn't occur to them! But, yes, she was young, and her spirit was far from doused just because a tall, lean stranger had happened along with noble conservation ideas.

Erratically flicking a duster, she was faced with the bitter realisation that Brance was not now threatened with eviction from his cosy cabin on Davis property. If anything, his position was strengthened, for there was no doubt he would only gain favour in her father's eyes when he learned that it was Brance who had encouraged the absentee lumberjacks back to work.

Lindsey didn't see Nick all week, but on Friday she received a message from the Mollenda household. It came in the form of a short note written on crested paper requesting Miss Davis's presence for afternoon tea, and was signed *Los Senhores Mollenda*.

Lindsey put on a neat sun-dress for the occasion. She had visited the sugar estates in the past in a neighbourly way, but on this particular afternoon she was struck by the formal atmosphere of the household.

The sugar-cane fields stretched as far as the eye could see in any direction. In their midst was the grand old mansion, balconied, festooned with greenery and steeped in an air of the past.

Flowering clay urns had been placed on either side of the doorway. She was received by a soft-footed servant who led her into a room filled with fine furniture and Portuguese lace. After a few moments he returned. This time she was shown into a salon where two immense sofas dominated the interior. Between was a table laid out elegantly with everything required for afternoon refreshments.

Gregorio Mollenda was a man whose frail frame barely supported him on foot, but he rose gallantly from the sofa at Lindsey's entry. She was reminded of Nick when he smiled, though his features were more finely drawn and less inclined to ruthlessness around the mouth. His wife greeted her warmly and invited her to pour tea for them all. This was an honour which Lindsey performed steadily. It was a little unnerving to be sitting alone on a huge sofa across from an elderly couple who seemed to watch her every movement with interest.

She made small talk while she passed round the fancy cakes, and they listened. She knew that there were three daughters in the family. They had all been married off to suitable husbands and seldom visited the mansion except for holidays. This made a fairly lengthy topic of conversation asking after each one, and of course the grandchildren.

Somehow this got her on to her own childhood, a subject which the couple couldn't get enough of. They

wanted to know all about her education and
background in England. They were proud but gentle
souls, and Lindsey liked them despite a certain hauteur
in their manner. But with every new talking point she
kept wishing that Nick would appear.

Curiously the son of the household was never
mentioned. After the tea, Gregorio rose and shuffled off
in a dignified way to his own quarters. In another room
Madame Mollenda opened a carved chest and showed
her fine lacework bedspreads and tablecloths worked
by the fingers of long-gone female members of the
family. When it was time to go, she presented Lindsey
with a small lace handkerchief embroidered with the
family crest, which later, in the sunny outdoors, smelled
faintly of age.

She arrived back at Springlands flushed faced and a
little keyed up. Ben greeted her absently when she
entered the house. 'Well,' she laughed jerkily, 'aren't
you going to ask me how I fared over tea with the
senior Mollendas?'

'Nick was here,' he said in a somewhat dazed way.

'He was?' She laughed again, this time incredulously.
'There was me sitting under the family magnifying glass
thinking he was out on the sugar estates and would be
popping in anytime to give me some moral support. No
wonder he never showed up.'

Her forced gaiety petered out then, and she eyed her
father curiously. 'You look as if you've had a shock of
some sort. Why was Nick here?'

In the same dazed way Ben replied, 'He wants to buy
the southland timber stretch.'

'He wants to buy it!' Lindsey echoed blankly. But
after the first wave of surprise had passed, she
brightened excitedly, 'But that's wonderful! I always
knew Nick was a solid friend to have around. He knows

you'll never be able to cut the timber and he wants to help us in some way. I think that's marvellous for him to make an offer like that.'

Her father nodded. 'It's not a fortune, but properly invested it could accumulate into a nice little nest-egg for you when you're older.'

'Forget about me,' she said impatiently. 'We could use the money to set up some other kind of timber trade once we're through at Tacana Hill. You said yes, of course?'

At his non-committal air she became more impatient. 'Dad, don't tell me you're dithering over a wonderful opportunity like this? We've got the men and the machines. Once the creditors are paid off we might even be able to hire out our services to other logging concerns. What's the point of holding on to something that's not going to do us any good?'

'Sentimental reasons, I suppose,' he smiled. 'These lands have belonged to a distant branch of my family— and yours—for hundreds of years.'

'We can't put a wedge of earth on our plates to eat,' she said practically, 'and we can't have the wood. If we want to survive wouldn't it be better to cut down on some of our land?'

As though half in agreement with this Ben sighed and said, 'I told Nick I'd think it over for a while.'

Lindsey had to be satisfied with that.

But all over the weekend she felt exhilarated by the turn of events. Thanks to Nick helping them out of their dilemma, she could show Brance Mackenzie that, far from going under because of his tiresome ideals, the Davis Logging Company would shortly be thriving the same as ever.

And his days on Springlands property were certainly numbered now. Nick had a chronic dislike of the forestry man and would waste no time in asking him to leave.

On Sunday afternoon she was feeling so elated that she decided to plan a banquet-type meal for the evening. Usually when Zina was in town, Lindsey relied on cooked left-overs and scratch meals to see them through until Monday. But tonight, she decided, would be something of an occasion. After all, it wasn't every day that one could think of being solvent again after weeks of wandering on the brink of poverty.

She was well on the way to producing a tasty three-course affair, with pans bubbling and the oven going, when a shadow fell across the kitchen doorway. She jumped, not because she was nervous at being alone in the house; it was the sight of Brance which jerked all her senses alive.

Feebly, she schooled that sweet ache of pleasure which always drained her whenever he was near. And, exasperatedly, she knew she had not tucked him away at the corners of her life as expertly as she had thought. But she was working on it. Though her hands trembled holding the dicing knife, she was working on it.

'It's customary to knock before entering a private household,' she said unwelcomingly.

'I did. Almost splintered the door,' he joked. 'I couldn't see anyone around, but the action seemed to be in here so I . . . kind of followed my nose.'

She knew he was sniffing the mixed aromas appreciatively and ignored his approval. He added at the lack of response, 'I came to see Ben. Not laid up, is he?'

'Far from it. Sam's taken him fishing over at Potema Creek, so it looks like you've had a wasted trip.'

'Oh, I don't know,' he shrugged. 'The light will be failing soon. They can't hook anything in the dark. Maybe I'll wait.'

'You're likely to get very bored,' she said hintingly. 'I'm sure what you have to say to my father will keep.'

'I think it's important enough to hang on.' He didn't take the hint, but rather startled her then by adding lazily, 'Seems your visit to the old Mollenda property the other day has caused quite a stir among the work-force on the estate. The cane cutters see so little glamour in their lives they're full of how the English lady came to take tea with their ageing overlords, and are now gaily putting two and two together.'

Colouring slightly over her task, Lindsey said acidly, 'I didn't know there were any forests of note on the Mollenda property to add to your fat list of takeovers.'

'Nope,' he replied evenly. 'But there is a very nasty case of moth-borer running rife in the sugar-cane. Apparently Nick Mollenda passed on my information about the new pesticide to his overseer. But the poor guy's so worried, he sought me out for more information and advice. He wanted me to see the extent of the damage, so I've been making one or two trips to help out. As a matter of fact I've just come from there.'

'Apart from the moth-borer there's a very nasty case of self-importance around here,' Lindsey carped. 'Nick knows how to run his sugar estates. Are you telling me that he calmly stood by and let you interfere on his land?'

'He doesn't know anything about my visits,' came the reply. 'From what I hear, he makes the occasional tour of inspection of the cane-fields to placate the old folks, And of course he sees to it that nobody gets a chance to rest on his machete, or whatever, if he can help it. But the greater part of his working day he spends in a private office he has well away from the house where sugar, it seems, is by no means his main business interest.'

Lindsey digested this information before replying. She had often though that Nick was unusually successful as a sugar grower. Though she was his immediate neighbour she had never really been sure how he made use of his time on the estates. It irked her that Brance, a stranger to these parts, should know more than she did, so she responded with a tart smile, 'You always end up playing the administering angel don't you? You come here wreaking havoc on honest, hard-working people on behalf of your precious organisation, then make out you can't help everybody enough.' She attacked an egg she needed with a mixing fork. 'It's a good job some of us know who our friends are around here.'

He had moved to the table alongside where she was working to examine a fruit trifle she had recently creamed over. 'It's easy in my job to make enemies,' he murmured mildly, 'but they don't usually have corn-silk hair and a figure that looks good in forest gear.'

The masculine timbre of his voice twanged on her taut nerves. Tremblingly, she had never been more conscious of his maleness than she was now here in the domestic confines of the kitchen. Though she had not allowed her eyes to rest more than a second at a time in his direction, the finger of her memory could trace every outline of his weathered features, bronze-streaked and often unruly brown hair; his broad khaki-clad shoulders tapering down to lean hips and a lazy stance which in itself stirred her blood and sent it pulsing haphazardly through her veins.

If she was to be entirely honest with herself she wanted his kiss now, the feel of his mouth on hers, more than she had ever wanted anything in her life. So far gone was she in her desire to feel his arms crushing her close, the savage pressure of his lips on hers, she clutched liked a drowning person at the only thing that would save her.

'As I said,' her voice sounded strangely distant, as though coming from the tunnel of her self-control, 'I've always known who our friends are. And Dad is learning too.' She paused long enough to give her news sufficient build-up then crowed, 'Nick has offered to buy all our southland stretch of rain forests where we're forbidden to cut. So you see, thanks to his help the Davis Logging Company is no longer a dying concern.'

Naturally she turned then to see the effect of her words on Brance. It was disappointing. He was merely thoughtful while replying, 'An extremely benevolent gesture on the part of your neighbour.'

True he seemed pensive after that, but he didn't go as she had hoped. If anything he appeared intent on standing in as kitchen assistant, expertly passing the utensil she needed at exactly the right time. 'If you're angling after presenting yourself at the dinner table as an extra guest,' she said thinly, 'forget it. We've already got Sam staying and I don't cook for an army.'

He sniffed the aroma from a bubbling pan with pained delight and complained, 'I've been eating food out of a can for so long I've forgotten what a good meal tastes like.'

'What makes you think this one will be good?' she asked sourly.

'Well, you think a lot of your Dad and Sam so you're hardly likely to foul up all this loving labour just to get rid of me. And anyway, I can keep going on small helpings that might just go to waste.'

Against her better judgment, she decided he had talked himself into it. And while they kept up the banter, albeit on a knife-edge like this, she felt safe from the magnetism of his maleness which reached out and threatened her at every turn.

He offered to lay the dinner table and made a fair job

of it, carrying through trays of crockery, cutlery and glassware at her direction, with considerable ease. He was not short on a touch of imagination either. Robbing one of the window sills of a flowering plant, he swathed the pot at the base with a colourful table napkin and placed it in the centre of the table, where the pretty scarlet spray added a festive air to the lay-out.

When Ben and Sam arrived, they were delighted to find added male support in the shape of the forestry man. Men-like, they all sat down like hungry babies and waited for Lindsey to feed them.

Despite her cool reservations where Brance was concerned, and she would have been happier if her father had shown a little more distance after all the man had done to them, it was a rip-roaring occasion.

The older men bragged unashamedly about the size of the fish they had seen and *almost* caught in Potema Creek. Brance topped their unlikely stories with even taller ones about the weight and length of the Canadian river fish he had hooked in his time.

After supper he and her father closeted themselves away in his study-cum-office. Sam taught her how to play gin rummy. She won quite a few hands, which amused them both. Sam was her father's best friend. They had worked together around the world since being young men. And when Ben had inherited the lumber business he had asked his old buddy to join him. As his chief logger, Sam was knocking on in years now, but like her father he was tough, if a little grizzled. And he knew everything there was to know about felling trees. Having no family of his own, Lindsey was well aware, he regarded her with the same paternal affection that Ben did.

It was late when her father returned to the living-room. 'And now I suppose everybody wants a nightcap?' She rose in a mock, pained way for she had enjoyed seeing him aglow in the masculine company at the table. 'Ask Brance if he can stomach hot cocoa along with the rest of us.'

'Brance has gone,' Ben said. 'He asked me to pass on his goodnights to you both. He seemed to want to be off.'

Lindsey drifted towards the kitchen, fighting back a ridiculous disappointment. If she hated the man so, why should she care that they weren't all going to sit and cosily drink cocoa together?

While she was preparing the drinks, she cast her mind back over the evening. She recalled now that Brance had been thoughtful at times, despite projecting a playful air for the benefit of the two older men.

And why had he wanted to see her father?

Determined to find out, she waited until Sam had left, then put the question bluntly.

'He wanted my permission to do some experiments in the southland forests,' Ben replied easily enough.

'What kind of experiments?' Lindsey's eyes narrowed.

'He didn't go into detail, just said it was something to do with the plant life.'

At this she let out a breath. 'Can't you see he's just looking for an excuse to further his own ends? There are several very rare trees in those rain forests. If he takes a sample of every one it's going to be a feather in his cap.'

'Maybe,' Ben nodded. 'But I told him to go ahead anyway.'

Lindsey went to bed quietly fuming. That's what happened when a forestry man like Brance Mackenzie came along! Being in something of the same line of business, he was halfway to charming himself into her father's heart from the start.

At least, one eyebrow quirked darkly as she slid between the sheets, she *supposed* it was just because Brance was a tree man that he and her father got on so well together.

The following week was a busy one for Lindsey. There were trips to town to be made. Ben's leg was knitting nicely; he had had the stitches removed from the thigh gash, but Dr Loy wanted to line up a series of exercises which would have to be practised at home once the plaster cast was removed.

Besides the hospital trips, Lindsey visited the adjoining sugar estates whenever she had a free afternoon. The Mollenda couple had issued this open invitation over tea that day, and she had to admit to a certain curiosity where Nick was concerned. However, the outings turned out to be quite enjoyable and she saw nothing unusual in the way Nick ran the plantation.

True, the field workers cast wary glances his way while endeavouring to move at double speed whenever he was passing. But the mischievous smiles they gave her behind his back, were sunny and warm and she felt that she provided some small diversion from the monotony of their daily routine.

She and Nick usually toured the estate on horseback. It was exhilarating skirting the vast stretches of waving green cane leaves, white clouds scudding across the blue sky and the jungle-clad hillsides proving a luxuriant backcloth.

Nick showed her the sugar-mills where the juice was boiled and put through a complicated series of evaporation vessels.

Sometimes they would ride away from the work areas and stroll by the river. Bright plumed birds were common here. Lindsey had seen a gorgeous cock-of-the-rock, a winged specimen with a golden-yellow cape of feathers over black body and a high, black-fringed yellow crest. The bell-bird was not as flamboyant but his chiming song was distinctive. Whatever their shape or colour she never tired of the picture they made, skimming the water or adorning the trees.

She had often felt that she ought to thank Nick for his wonderful offer to buy their land. But he never mentioned the subject and somehow she found it difficult to broach herself. She wasn't sure if he would have preferred her father to say nothing of his generosity. This would be like Nick, so until the deal was through, she decided to reserve her thanks.

Another week drew to a close. Ben was now making trips to Tacana Hill and doing office work on the site. He did however spend a lot of his time resting his leg at Springlands. A growing restlessness in Lindsey prompted her to ask casually one afternoon when she returned from the sugar estate, 'Has Brance been around?'

'No. I haven't seen him for some time,' Ben looked up briefly from the logging sheets he was studying.

'Surely he's been giving his usual invaluable advice at the Tacana site?' she jeered, pathetically hopeful of a nod from her father.

There was none forthcoming. 'Not while I've been there,' he said. And he added meditatively, 'Come to think of it, I haven't heard anybody mention having seen him in the district lately.'

'He's probably divesting us of all our rare tree shoots in the rain forests.'

'Probably.' Missing the corrosive curl of her smile, Ben nodded vaguely and went back to eyeing his logging figures.

Lindsey told herself that of course she couldn't care

less if Brance didn't drop in at Springlands now and then. She had arranged her life neatly and to suit herself. All in all things were progressing pleasantly.

Yet, despite her resolve to do otherwise, she spent most of her time wondering what had happened to the irritating forestry man. It wasn't like him to stay holed up with his job for almost three weeks. He had always made a practice of taking time out from his botanical pursuits to visit the people around the area. When Zina returned from one of her family weekends, she asked offhandedly if the forestry man had been seen in town. The answer was negative.

As time went on Lindsey took to waking up in a cold sweat in the middle of the night. Supposing Brance was in trouble? Supposing a rotting tree, or something, had fallen across him and he was miles away from help of any kind? There were swamps deep in the forest, she knew—or what if he had come off worst with an over-inquisitive wild beast!

When she could stand the torment no longer, she climbed into her logging run-about one morning and set out to investigate. Her father had gone with Sam at the wheel of the ranch-waggon to do a spot of work, so there would be no embarrassing questions to answer.

It was almost midday when she arrived at the region up-river. She had driven so madly she had whizzed past the trading store with only a wave for Danny Capucho.

She parked the run-about on the now disused logging site and set out through the trees. At every step she expected to come across a maimed khaki-clad figure lying on the ground. The silence was daunting. It seemed to bode the very worst. She listened for the heartening sounds of activity up ahead. There was nothing save the chatter and twitter of tree life.

Moving slowly and fearfully ahead she became so

limp with anxiety that her knees shook and the blood pounded in her ears. The sounds of the forest played tricks on her senses. She thought she heard calls for help in all directions. Every prone log catapulted her heart into her throat.

The first thing she noticed about the cabin when she came within sight of it, was its deserted air. Nearing it, she saw that the windows were shuttered and locked to keep out the wildlife. The door, too, had a padlock hanging from the clasp.

So that was it! The tears that filled her eyes may have been of pure relief. But there was anger too, in the way they flashed in the sunlight. Now she knew why Brance Mackenzie hadn't been seen round the district lately. He had gone, sloped off, lit out, taking with him the rare tree cuttings and botanical specimens from Springlands that would further his career.

The black despair which engulfed her was frightening. She had spent these past weeks fighting to be rid of him, and now he had gone, it felt as though her heart had been pierced through with a knife and lay like a dead thing inside her.

But bitterness dried her tears. Well, what else did she expect? He had come here, caused havoc with his ban on timber production. But there was nothing to keep him here now that he had got what he wanted for himself out of the wreckage.

She drove back to the trading store and drowned her pique in a drink with Danny. His partner was there, a plump individual with a deep belly laugh despite his shrewd countenance. Lindsey joined in the gaiety but only from the outside of the prickly hurt that encased her. Men! she told herself, the memory of the padlocked cabin burned on her brain. They were all the same.

\* \* \*

The days drifted by and Lindsey drifted along with them. It wasn't that she was at a loose end. She had the sugar plantation to while away the time in, hadn't she? And Nick's company almost every day. Nick, who was always expensively groomed, even on horseback. Studying him privately when they were together, she reminded herself often what a handsome figure of a man he made in the somewhat bucolic surroundings of the cane fields; one that any woman would be gratified to have as a companion. If there was a sharpness to his smile, a ruthlessness in his attitude to the humble field workers, she forced herself to see only his attentiveness towards her, his concern for her well-being. These qualities, she was sure, more than made up for the darker facets of his nature.

The great day came when Ben had his plaster cast removed. He, Sam, herself and Zina had a little supper party at Springlands to celebrate the event. But Lindsey felt jaded somehow, and turned in early to bed.

She drove her father daily now over to the Tacana logging site and wandered off on her own, gazing up and around at the giant mora and crabwood, leafy greenheart and wallaba without seeing them.

There was nothing Ben liked more than to rough it with his men in the logging camps. Lindsey would occasionally stay to lunch too and join the queue with tin plate and mug for helpings of stew and coffee. Annoyingly, visions of another camp site with dripping clothes on the line and stew by the fire would make her throat ache. Then, resolutely, to prove to herself that she had no fear of getting indigestion where absconding forestry men were concerned, she would queue for another helping—of coffee at least.

If she was to be honest with herself, food interested her little these days. She knew she had lost weight, was

inclined to be irritable. Perhaps her father noticed her
peaky look, but it was Sam who had the face to
mention it.

'A few weeks ago you were blooming like a freshly
sprinkled rosebud,' his affection for her softened his
grizzled aspect, and his logger's tongue. 'Now it's as
though someone's spread weed-killer around. What's
ailing ye, child?'

'The only thing bothering me is old timber types
trying to wax poetic when they should be getting on
with the job.'

As soon as the words were out, she wanted to cut her
tongue out. The hurt in his rheumy old eyes made her
rush to plant a kiss on his stubbly cheek. 'I'm fine,
Sam,' she smiled wanly to atone for her waspish
behaviour. 'Just in need of a change, I guess.'

The change came in a way that she least expected,
although if she had given enough thought to her
afternoons on the Mollenda estate she might have
regarded it as a natural sequence of things. In any case,
as soon as she received the news she returned home
flush-faced in search of her father. He was taking his
exercise in the garden, using a stick to assist his weak
leg. Happy to see him almost mobile again, she asked,
'Do you think you'll be all right in Zina's care for a
while?' And rushing on with a laugh, 'Nick wants to
take me to Georgetown for a few days.'

'And you're going?' Ben said, with not quite the
enthusiasm that she had expected.

'Well of course! It's just what I need, a break from
the logging business. A chance to sniff some sea
breezes, to do some shopping.'

'That's not what I mean,' he eyed her keyed-up state
with fatherly insight. 'I mean, you're going with Nick?'

'That's right,' she said lightly, tensed for argument. 'I

think you mentioned him to me more than once in the past as an eligible type.'

'And I seem to recall you saying that you saw him as anything but a prospective husband.'

Cross with her father for bringing this up. Cross with herself because she had no convincing reply. Cross at the whole world for no reason, she snapped, 'Why have you turned against Nick? The two of you have always been reasonably good friends.'

'I haven't turned against Nick,' Ben shrugged. 'He made us a wonderful offer for the southlands tract which I'm thinking of taking him up on . . .'

'You are?' she glowed. But any real pleasure she might have got from this statement was stymied by his reluctance to add anything more.

Biting her lip, she transferred her gaze to a plumbago bush. Oh, he didn't need to put it into words. She knew he missed Brance. She knew he had been hurt at his going off without a word. In his tough, taciturn way he had kept his disappointment to himself. But he couldn't hide it from Lindsey who would have preferred not to guess any of his secret feelings.

## CHAPTER FIVE

GEORGETOWN, with its nineteenth-century wooden houses supported on stilts, its green boulevards laid along the lines of the old Dutch canals, has a charm of its own.

Lindsey had visited the capital once or twice in the old days with her father when she had been keen to see as much of the country as possible.

There was everything in the East Indian shops, from beaten brassware and gold and silver Indian jewellery, to stuffed alligators, guava jelly, and Amerindian curios.

But the markets, the zoo, and the back streets she had explored in those days were a far cry from the places she visited with Nick.

Expensive nightspots were a must on his programme. He was a member of various exclusive clubs and every day they went to the racecourse.

At first she had been excited at the colour and animation of a Georgetown race meeting. But she soon became privately horrified at the vast amounts of money which Nick lost on the Tote. Her visits then became a source of secret anxiety until one afternoon he recouped a small fortune by putting his money on an outsider.

The ups and downs of what appeared to be his main pastime in Georgetown, she personally could have done without. And one afternoon something happened which left her emotionally in shreds in another way.

They were in their usual exclusive box with an excellent view of the winning post. People milled around near the rail, but being in an elevated position Nick could watch his favourite's progress up the flat. Lindsey had got to the point where her mind wandered, and her gaze began to idle over the crowd. It was then that she saw Brance.

He was taller than most, in a white open-necked shirt which emphasised his tanned physique. The joyous stab which weakened her knees as her glance fell on him was soon tempered by an angry hurt and a peevishness. So this was what he was getting up to these days!

Having spent a good many weeks first ruining her father and then battening on him, he was now living it up for a while before, no doubt, moving on to his next prey—some unsuspecting logger in another part of the country.

And his habits hadn't changed either, she saw sourly over a harshness in her throat.

He was still whiling away his free time in the company of attractive women. The one he had with him this afternoon, had sunset gold hair and a kind of sweet maturity. Smartly dressed with a little pill-box hat topping her french pleat, she laughed a lot in excitement at the race, and Brance's smile for her was sloping and virile.

Lindsey was glad that Nick, having watched his horse take second place, was sufficiently satisfied to suggest that they leave.

Driving back to town, she put on an air of having enjoyed the whole thing while her insides were torn with so many conflicting emotions she felt drained.

Of course it was better that Brance had gone out of their lives. And what was it to her that women found him so boorishly attractive? She certainly felt nothing for him but an abject hate after what he had done to them. If, at the root of her being, something cried out to be heard, she made a supreme effort to ignore it.

True, she felt a misery so deep it was like a malady that robbed her of vitality. But she would ignore it. *She would.*

That evening Nick was especially attentive. They danced in a popular nightclub, and Lindsey told herself often that he was one of the most striking men in the room.

Later under the stars, in amorous mood, he kissed her long and lingeringly and, moved as any woman might be when starved of what she most desired, she responded almost avidly.

Caressing her absently with his lips, Nick's mind wandered on to other things. 'When we get back to Springlands,' he said, 'I'll have to press for an answer from your father on my offer to take those stagnant southside forests off his hands. He's a proud man, but he can't run a business on pride.'

So he had guessed that she knew about his proposition? With relief she was eager to discuss the subject now. 'I think he realises that,' she smiled. 'He told me before we came away that he's more or less made up his mind to sell.'

'He has?' Nick's eyes glowed darkly. He lowered his gaze and took to fingering the strands of her hair. 'I'm happy for you sake, Lindsey,' he said. 'I know what you've been through these past weeks.'

She nodded. 'It has been something of a nightmare.'

'There's no doubt that that Mackenzie fellow dealt the Davis Company a crippling blow, but in a way I'm glad,' he drew her to him, 'because the trouble has brought you and me closer together.'

She gazed up at him then, her eyes shining with gratitude. 'Nick, you've been so wonderful about everything,' she murmured. 'I'd like you to know that Dad and I will never be able to thank you enough for being such a good friend to us in our time of need.'

'Friend?' he sloped a dark eyebrow. 'I hope after tonight you and I will regard ourselves as two people much, much closer than that.'

While she lowered her lashes shyly he reached into his pocket. Her heart gave a sudden lurch when she saw the small velvet box he had placed in her hand. However she had long since decided to ignore that part of her anatomy, and radiantly she exclaimed on opening the box, 'Oh Nick! It's beautiful!'

The ring was a large square emerald surrounded by

diamonds. Of course she didn't know enough about gems to assess if they were real or paste, but it was certainly a striking-looking ring and fitted well on her finger. And after all, that was what counted most.

Nick kissed her to seal their engagement. 'This will be no surprise to my parents,' he revealed. 'They're anxious to see me . . . domesticated,' he smiled. Taking his glance to the hand that now wore his ring he added, 'I hope you will feel able to make them happy by agreeing to an early wedding?'

'Early? How early?' she asked a little breathlessly.

'Within the next few days,' he shrugged.

Once again her heart lurched down a step at the momentum at which she was being carried along. Yet she couldn't say she was really surprised. Nor would she say that Nick's proposal was anything other than what she desired herself.

'If that's the way you want it, Nick,' she smiled up at him. 'Then I'll be only too glad to give them the happiness they deserve.'

The days that followed were paradoxically lonely ones for Lindsey. Nick had lots of business to attend to in the city, and most of the time she spent seeing the sights or seeking respite from the heat and the humidity by lying naked under a cool sheet in her hotel bedroom.

In the evening they went to the usual night spots, but Nick was preoccupied a lot of the time with what had taken place between him and business acquaintances during the day. And if the truth were known Lindsey was becoming jaded with the racy atmosphere of the capital. She longed to be back in deep country up river, where the only flamboyance came from the colourful parrots in the rain forests, and the night noises nothing worse than the insect life in the grounds of Springlands.

Thankfully, Nick was needed on the sugar estates and the day when they finally started out on the return journey, Lindsey experienced both relief and a slight uneasiness. Throughout the long drive she was conscious of the ring on her finger. Heavy, almost ornate, it could not be missed, not by any stretch of the imagination.

She could of course slip it off later, but she decided flatly against this. It was best that things stayed out in the open. Or, to put it another way, the sooner her new status was accepted the better.

After building up to something of an emotional pitch on the drive it was a considerable anticlimax to arrive at Springlands and find no one at home.

Nick dropped her off and drove on, and hawking her light travel bag inside she found the living-room empty and Zina pottering around in the kitchen as usual.

At the sight of her the ebony face split into a smile of sorts. 'Well, don't tell me I'm going to have someone to cook for around here? I've spent most of the week giving my table spreads to the birds.'

'Where's Dad?' Lindsey asked curiously.

'Ever since he's been walking on two legs,' came the dry reply, 'he's gone back to his old ways of bedding down with his men in the logging camp. I haven't seen him in three days.'

Lindsey went off to unpack. She needed a bath, and anyway it was too late to start out today. Tomorrow she would drive over to Tacana Hill and get it over with once and for all, with her father.

Cruising through familiar country the next morning, her joy at being back in the bush was clouded by the family meeting that was looming. She was, after all, of an age where she could please herself, so what was there to feel gloomy about?

Amid the noise and clamour at the logging site she searched for her father and came upon Sam. He was shovelling near a pile of chips for the pulp mills. He asked her how her trip had been, spat out a coin of tobacco juice, and said with a sideways glance, 'Brance is back. Bin back three or four days.'

Lindsey went hot and cold at the news. 'Don't tell me we haven't got rid of him for good?' she said harshly, while the electric thrill of knowing he was in the district culminated in a singing which she convinced herself was in her ears, not in her heart.

'Nope,' Sam said. 'Seems he's been at the coast doing some research.'

'I can guess,' Lindsey sneered to herself. She had seen the kind of research which had kept him busy. It wore a pill-box hat and a very fetching pink outfit.

Sam leaned on his shovel and slapped his thigh. 'Had some nights, Ben and me, chawing with him round the camp fire at his log cabin. Sat the stars out more than once, and Brance keeps a well-stocked whisky shelf along with his vittles,' he added slyly.

'Very cosy,' Lindsey grated. 'And where is my father now?'

'I left him at the cabin and came on here to do a spot of graft,' Sam spat on his palms and took up his shovel again. 'Reckon he'll show up when he's ready.'

'Well when he does, just tell him I'm back.' With this message to her father she returned to her runabout. If he thought she was going to search him out on the territory where Brance had his cabin, he was going to have to wait a long time! She drove away in a flurry of dust. In any case, she had a wedding to prepare for.

News of her coming marriage to Nick soon spread around the district. Many of the cane cutters had their homes alongside the river, and nothing travels faster in the bush than word of mouth.

Lindsey had decided to wear a white lace dress for the ceremony, to be held in the Mollenda mansion. Nick's parents were very catholic in their tastes and proud by nature, and the dress, full-skirted and knee-length, was not new, but had been seldom worn.

She was eyeing the scant show of flowers in the garden one afternoon with a view to fashioning herself a bouquet when the ranch-waggon appeared with her father at the wheel.

If there was a degree of strain on both sides at the reunion, an onlooker would not have noticed. Lindsey ran to kiss her father and laughingly he held her in a bear-hug for a while, then companionably they made for the indoors.

She helped Zina lay a special tea-table beside the window in the living-room. Avoiding the subject on both their minds, they talked mainly about the sights to be seen in Georgetown. Lindsey didn't know if the news had travelled as far as the logging camp. She saw the way Ben's eyes were drawn to the ring on her hand. Then stirring his tea deliberately he said, 'I'm not selling our timber lands to Nick, Lindy. Brance has advised me against it.'

She heard his words and felt her face becoming white and pinched as they percolated through to her brain. 'What,' she asked, her voice low with anger, 'has Brance Mackenzie got to do with the Davis Logging Company?'

'We might have cause to thank him,' Ben shrugged. 'From what he tells me we can make a comfortable living just exporting the plants in those rain forests for medicinal and nutritional purposes.'

Lindsey couldn't believe her ears. 'You can't be

trying to tell me that you're going to turn down an offer which would put us on our feet again as a business, and try and scrape along on a pittance from wild plants?' She gave a cracked laugh to add ridicule to her reply.

'I happen to think it's a sound idea, Lindy,' Ben said, his own face serious. 'According to Brance we've got a wealth of stuff which in one form or another is used to combat ailments in the world. Besides which, there's such things as the wild relatives of food crops which are valuable as new disease-resistant strains.'

'Brance! Brance!' she blazed sarcastically. 'I don't know how you ever managed without his profound advice. He's certainly charming everything you ever had from under your nose.'

Because she loved her father, she felt contrite enough then to say with a straight look, 'I suppose you know what this kind of a decision is going to do to Nick and me at a time like this?'

Ben met her gaze squarely. 'My mind's made up, Lindy,' he said. 'I'm not selling, and that's that.'

It was his rank determination not to be swayed which filled Lindsey's eyes with tears of a new fury. 'Well, don't discuss it with me, will you?' she carped. 'As long as you and Brance have it all cut and dried, who else matters?' Her chair clattered over as she jumped up. 'But one thing's for sure, Dad. There's one Davis in this family who *can* see the wood for the trees, and if you won't, I aim to weed out that unwanted forestry type before we all end up on the breadline!'

Blazing a trail from the living-room to the outdoors with her pique, she flung herself into her father's ranch-waggon for speed—well, it was time he rested up at the house anyway—and shot away.

On the drive, she kindled the flames of her hatred by going over in her mind all the troubles which had

befallen her and her father since the arrival of Brance
Mackenzie.

The jungle greenery whizzed by. Honeycreepers,
bobolinks and scarlet macaws fluttered up in fright at her
passing. Creeks and rapids of the river were left behind
as she bumped and bounced along, teeth set, to her
destination.

The log cabin was deserted when she got there. But
contrary to her last visit here, the door was open and
there was every sign that its occupant was spreading
himself amid a nice supply of home comforts.

A wood fire burned merrily just outside the doorway.
Tin pans and coffee pot were arranged neatly around
the embers. A short distance away, a line was hung with
freshly washed clothes.

Inside the stove was lit to take the dank forest chill
off the room—or was it to protect the precious plant
shoots potted and labelled on the trestle table?

Her eyes fastened on the methodical display and all
at once the rows and rows of green and flowering
specimens became the focus of her loathing and crazy,
mixed-up love for Brance.

Without wasting time searching for ways to get
even with him she raised an arm and in one sweeping
motion sent the entire contents of the trestle table
tumbling to the floor. Crushed shoots, splintered
marker pegs, chipped containers made a satisfying pile
amid scattered earth, and being of a tidy mind she
was scooping up the debris and idly tossing it out of
the nearest window when Brance's frame darkened
the doorway.

In two strides he was jerking her away from her task
with such force she was almost spun across the room.
'You've just signed yourself on as plant picker for the
rest of the daylight hours,' he growled, his lips white.

'Have you any idea what you've done, laying your peevish little hands on a collection of this kind?'

Now that all the exhilaration of hitting back had passed, the bare earth-strewn table did look a little forlorn. But Lindsey tossed her head to rid herself of any feelings of guilt. 'What I've done,' she snapped, breathing hard, 'is nothing to the damage you've inflicted since you and your pious conservation ideas arrived in these parts.'

'Your trouble is you're too pig-headed to accept change,' his own breathing was far from even. 'Admit it. You've got as much a soft spot for these trees as I have, but you're too damned cussed to let it show.'

'Oh, change is all right so long as the great Brance Mackenzie is dictating it, is that it?' She ignored his comment about the trees. 'Well, since we're on the subject of change, it seems to me the best one for all concerned at the moment would be for you to move on and leave my father to make his own decisions on what to do with the miles of forests we now have on our hands.'

'So that's what's biting you.' The suggestion of a taut grin peeped through his wrath. 'Well, I've been expecting a visit, but none of your she-cat tantrums are going to change common sense. Too bad if it doesn't fit in with your present scheme of things.'

Oh, she knew what he meant by this last remark. The quality of his expression made it perfectly obvious.

'Don't worry,' she raised her chin. 'Nick and I will go ahead and marry regardless of you tainting my father's mind against my future husband.'

'He's in a mighty big hurry to tie the knot, isn't he?' Brance drawled. 'Must have been an illuminating trip to Georgetown.'

'Our engagement was a foregone conclusion,' she said

airily. 'And we both discovered that we were of the same mind in not wanting to prolong the pre-marital period. How was your trip?'

'Edifying,' he said. 'I made one or two interesting discoveries myself.'

Lindsey had the uncomfortable feeling that he was referring to Nick in some obscure way. But thinking mainly of his female acquaintances scattered far and wide she purred, 'What a pity they didn't keep you at the coast indefinitely.'

'I reckoned I ought to get back,' he sloped an odd smile. 'The cable I was hanging on for, verifying one or two queries of mine, I can just as well pick up in town when it arrives.'

'I can't think what could have been so pressing here,' she smiled equally mirthlessly. 'Unless it was your keenness to influence my father against a perfectly good business deal.'

'I like Ben,' he reached for a flower root lying pathetically crumpled on the table. 'Unlike his daughter, he doesn't have a one-track view of things. If I can help him, I will.'

'I somehow don't see him being eternally grateful for the suggestion of setting up as plant farmer,' she sneered.

'Maybe he will, maybe he won't,' Brance's gaze was lowered over the crushed flower. Then, tossing it at her, he clipped, 'Time you were getting to work.'

Lindsey caught the flower against her bosom. She stared down at it and then at him and quivered rebelliously, 'You can't make me grovel around in the dirt for your absurd posies.'

'No?' He quirked one eyebrow devilishly. Nervously she watched him walk outside. Following, she saw him stride over to the ranch-waggon. What he dismantled from under the bonnet she didn't know, but it was small enough and apparently vital enough for him to toss playfully in his hand while he said with a grim smile, 'You don't move from here until that table is lined with specimens the same as when you went in there.'

## CHAPTER SIX

SWALLOWING, Lindsey glanced about her. 'But . . . there are snakes aren't there, and . . . well, I mean . . . live things out there?'

'I shouldn't worry,' he shrugged idly. 'There may be the odd serpent sleeping in a tree, but you leave him alone and he won't bother you.'

His careless attitude inflamed her. 'I see. As long as you get your potting shed refurbished, it doesn't matter if there's a few dead bodies strewn around in the process.'

'You're wasting time,' he hardened. 'There's the pretty heap you've made under the window. Sift out the ruined plants, match them up with those growing hereabouts in the forest and rescue what containers you can to hold them.'

She stood where she was, fuming with resentment. As a hint, he began to toss the vital engine part rhythmically in his hand.

When she could stand his sickening display of power no longer, she flung herself into action and muttered, 'Well, what do I use, my nail file?'

It was a feeble joke, of course, because she had simply rushed out of the house in what she stood up in, lounging slacks and a primrose shirt.

'You'll find a trowel and bucket at the side of the cabin,' he said.

She grabbed these utensils, scooped up a pile of crushed specimens, and stumped off hoping an anaconda or something would carry her off, and then he would be sorry.

Picking a spot a nice, safe short distance away she worked in this furious, fatalistic mood. Maybe the animal life in these forests remained hidden for the most part from the human eye, but she knew that there were ocelot here, and tapir and giant lizards, and it would serve him right if——

Suddenly she stopped digging and froze. Her glance had caught a movement in the bush immediately to her right. She had a feeling something had frozen there too and, looking straight into a white face which was staring at her through the leaves, she let out a piercing scream which sent the wild-life within a radius of half a mile running for cover.

Brance dropped what he was doing by the fire and covered the distance between them at a sprint. His face white and tense, he grabbed her away from the danger area. 'What's wrong?' Then watching the waving bushes as something scuttled off, squealingly and frantically into the distance, he let out a long, slow breath. 'It's only a bush pig.'

Lindsey should have felt ridiculous, but she didn't. Crushed against his protective frame she could hear his heart thudding—with what? Had it been fear for her safety?

With something like bemused power herself now, she raised her eyes to his. The look she saw there made her bones melt. Before she knew what was happening they were fused as one, her lips straining for fulfilment as hungrily as his own mouth sought contact.

Never had an embrace been so wild, so tumultuous, so full of primaeval yearnings that made these ancient forests appear like yearling glades in comparison. Drained from the sheer, sweet torment of it, Lindsey forced herself away from him at last. Eyeing the flowery specimen she still clutched in her hand she asked shakily as though out of interest, 'What's this plant called?'

'That's a rosy periwinkle,' he said hoarsely.

'And that blue one over there?' She had to do something to find firm ground for her feet.

'A relative of the cotton family.' His fingers trembling he took the root from her hand. 'Look, you've got to scoop them out keeping as much of their natural soil round the base as you can.'

'Yes, Brance,' she stooped with him as he demonstrated.

'Pass me a container,' he nodded to the pile. 'I'll show you how to tamp them down ... That's fine. Here, now try this wild maize flower.'

They soon had a system going where Brance was doing most of the digging. But Lindsey walked the long distances to and from the trestle table in the cabin, lining up the new specimens.

It was a way of channelling one's energies into less soul-searing activities; schooling one's perilously heightened senses into listening to reason. And gradually as ice-cold sanity returned, annoyance flooded in at the way she had just capitulated against him. She was really going to have to do something about the forestry man! Here she was engaged to Nick, yet just a touch from Brance and she became liquid fire in his arms.

They worked until the light faded. Perhaps the display was not as professional as the original rows of potted flora, but Lindsey considered it wasn't bad.

'I'll have that piece of engine now,' she held out her hand in the cabin doorway.

Moving out into the open Brance strolled a pace, turned, then patting his hip he said, 'It stays right where it is in my pocket.'

Lindsey stood rigid. From chalk white her face changed to an angry pink as the realisation struck her. 'You never intended to give it back to me, did you? You had me grovelling in the dirt over your precious nursery and all the while you knew you were going to hang on to that thing you have of mine.'

'That's right,' he said lazily.

Quivering with mortification and a very real fear of her own treacherous feelings, she croaked, 'You can't propose to keep me here for the night!'

'That's what I do propose.'

Drowningly, she blustered, 'Nick will have something to say about that.'

'I don't think Nick will want to know, once he hears that you've spent the night with me.'

'You wouldn't . . .!' she said faintly.

'Wouldn't I?' He crouched to stir up the fire and put the supper pans on the heat. 'If I have to stop you marrying someone out of sheer juvenile pique and cussedness, I shall.'

Lindsey felt limp, but obliged to battle. 'It will be your word against mine, of course.' She made an attempt to sound haughty.

'I don't think explanations will come into it,' he said easily. 'The scandal will be enough to finish you in the eyes of the Mollenda family. I've met the old couple. A charming pair, but riddled with the old conventions. Once they hear that you spent the night with me, holed up out here in the earthy wilds of my log cabin, any future contact with your neighbours is going to be mighty frosty indeed.'

'I can't believe that anyone could be so vile,' she glowered.

'Oh, it's no effort,' he said cheerfully. 'And in case you're thinking I won't have laid it on thick enough when I make sure the scandal breaks, don't forget, you and I spent a night together once before. And I can, if you push me, explain that night right down to the last detail . . . lacy underwear hanging on my line, for instance.'

Blushing furiously, she swung her back on him. Hands clenching and unclenching, she desperately wanted to show him that she was not as helpless as he thought. While her mind raced, his voice floated over to her, 'By the way, I've also put my jeep out of action, so that's little point in your trying to make a dash for it.'

She knew then that she was his prisoner for the night. The only thing to do now was to play it as cool as he was doing. She sauntered over to the fire. He had floured two fish, obviously caught in the river; the smell of them frying made her mouth water.

Just to let it be known that she didn't intend to go hungry this time, she lined up a tin plate and mug for herself once the meal was ready.

While they were eating, Brance said chattily, 'You know, I never did discover why you were so keen to sail that home-made raft down river.'

'I was trying to prove to my father that timber felled in these parts could be floated cost free as far as the saw-mill. But you nicely spiked all that, so it ceases to have any significance.'

He ignored her caustic smile and mused aloud, 'Springlands is big country, but there couldn't have been enough timber here to support full tree clearance over a long period.'

'As a matter of fact,' she enlightened him, 'logging was only started in these forests some ten years before my father came into the property.'

He nodded. 'And I bet they razed everything to the ground. In Canada we have a rule. For every tree that falls to the chain saw we plant one, or two saplings where space allows. If Ben's predecessors had worked in this way, his logging company would still have had plenty of timber to go at.'

'You can't know everything when you first take up a new occupation,' Lindsey defended her father's lack of foresight also, in this respect. 'We've been replanting for some years now and there will be forests in these parts again one day.'

They drained the coffee pot, after which Brance dug in his pockets for cigarettes. Lindsey drew on hers, watching the picture he made lounging meditatively across the fire from her, one long, jean-clad leg propped up to support his cigarette hand. His denim shirt was faded from many camp washings. Open at the chest, it emphasised his tough, lean physique; his nut-brown profile in the firelight.

She lowered her lashes and hung on to her cigarette. She wanted to talk about something, anything, but her throat felt too tight to get a word out. She tried to concentrate her attention on the sounds of the forest. All this did was heighten the primitiveness of their surroundings, the absolute remoteness of their camp fire site from the outside world.

Though she tried to prolong it indefinitely, her cigarette ran out in the end. Brance rose, tossed his butt in the fire and said, 'I'm ready for turning in.'

Rapidly Lindsey consolidated her position by the fire. 'I think I'll just doze here,' she hedged brightly.

'I wouldn't recommend sleeping out of doors in these parts,' he drawled. 'I'll make up the camp bed.'

For long enough she heard him moving about inside

the cabin. She sat glued to the fire. Her fear of the snuffling night life was nothing compared to that which gripped her when she thought of her treacherous emotions.

The fire sank to red embers. When it began to ash over and her skin became damp she realised that Brance had no plans to fetch more wood tonight. She rose stiffly and crept towards the cabin. The smell of the stove warmth was inviting compared to the dank outdoors.

All was in darkness. She almost fell across the sleeping-bagged shape stretched across the doorway inside.

Brance shot out a bare arm from his blankets to steady her. Contact with his flesh sent an electric quiver through her. 'I'm terribly sorry. I hope I didn't wake you,' she choked idiotically.

'You're frozen to the bone,' he grated, letting go of her at once. 'Get to bed and get some sleep.'

'Yes, Brance.' With crazy tears in her eyes she fumbled her way across to the camp bed. She undid buttons for comfort and slid between the sheets.

The darkness was broken only by the faint outline of the doorway facing on to the night. She could see the shape of Brance in his sleeping bag lying across it.

She closed her eyes; willing herself into a sleepy frame of mind was an exhausting pastime. She did everything she could to interest her brain in the idea of oblivion. And the more she worked at it, the more tense she became. Oh, she knew all too well where the snag lay. Her traitorous heart would not be fobbed off with simple slumber as an answer to its yearnings.

After what seemed hours of straining to relax, she heard Brance stir. Wide awake the same as she was, he was searching for some respite from total sleeplessness.

As he groped towards a pocket, she said in a small voice,' Brance, can I have a cigarette too?'

Without a word he felt his way across the interior towards her. Without a word too, Lindsey knew that her inner struggle was over. How, she asked her tussling principles, can you lie only yards away from the man you love and not want his touch? Just the brush of his hand against hers as he lit her cigarette would be better than this aching loneliness.

Her heart began to pound in her throat as he came beside the bed. She sat up, hoping her hand wouldn't shake when reaching towards his. She reminded herself that with only the dim light from the doorway nothing of her unsteady movements could be seen. Yet she felt that the whole room reverberated with her longing for Brance's nearness.

Bare-chested in the gloom, his jeans hugging his lean hips, he perched on the edge of the bed. She saw him hook one white cylinder between his lips. Heard him flick his lighter as he handed her the other.

Perhaps it was the tiny flame which ignited the touch-paper between them. Or perhaps it was the look each saw on the other's face in that flicker of illumination. They would never know, and neither cared. Tossing away cigarettes and lighter, Brance gave a groan and gathered her into his arms.

The pressure of his mouth on hers brought a moan too from Lindsey. It was as though she had been brought back from the gates of hell by his touch. A hell that was fast suffusing into a wondrous paradise.

Glorying in the wildfire of his passion, the scorching rapture of his lips on her throat, in the hollow of her breasts, all her hates and resentments melted in a love which craved, yearned, begged for fulfilment.

Her fingers, the palms of her hands roaming his bare

back, resorted to pressure in their urgency. She sank back among the pillows crushed by his bare chest, by his demanding lips, by her own overwhelming need of him.

Never had the ultimate joy been so close to being hers. Brance was all she would ever want in a man. To know his love was all she would ever ask in life.

She pressed him close to her. She could feel their wildly beating hearts as they fused as one.

Then suddenly, as though he had been shot, Brance lifted his head. She felt that his eyes were raking her in the gloom. She sensed also that they narrowed as unsteadily he drew away, a smile of sorts contorting his lips. 'Now wait a minute,' he breathed thickly. 'W.A.I.T. a cotton-picking minute!' And glinting at her. 'Why are you so warm, so soft, so pliable all at once? As if I didn't know! If you can't win with your she-cat tactics, there are other ways, is that it? You don't like the advice I've given your father to hold on to these forests and you think that you're going to soften me into changing my suggestion so that Nick can buy. Well, no deal, Lindsey. I happen to think it's the best move for Ben and none of your scheming ways is going to alter that.'

His words hit her like a sluicing of ice-cold water. She felt limp with shock, and helpless in the role she had fashioned for herself Always seething with hate in her dealings with him, always hotly resentful of his presence on Springlands property, how could she tell him now that such a thought had never entered her head? And how could she expect him to believe her?

The tears coursed down her cheeks as he moved across the room. When she had silently wiped away the last of her abysmal misery, she saw that he had draped down in the doorway and sat staring out into the night.

What wouldn't she have done for some excuse to drift penitently over there and smooth a hand over his unruly dark hair? But she had none, and sleep only came to assuaged minds.

A long time later, when a calmness had settled over the cabin she said in the darkness, 'Brance. Tell me about Canada. Your Canada.'

'My province is New Brunswick,' he replied easily. 'There's a little place called Sackville on the Westmorland coast. That's my home town. I grew up there. I can still smell the harness-shop near our timber home. If you didn't know one end of a work-horse from the other, your nose would lead you there. There's an old fellow sits in one corner of the store stitching horse collars by hand. Since no two horses are the same size or shape, he makes each collar to fit. He hasn't got much use for new shiny gadgets. Old Tom is a special friend of mine.'

He shifted his frame on the step and continued musing aloud. 'I went to Mount Allison university in Sackville. Tree-lined walks, even a lily-pond on the campus.' She felt that he grinned to himself in the dark. 'But it was some time before I took to studying timber seriously. Me and my buddies used to fish for salmon on the Miramichi river. In the old days of the log drives the river would be packed full of timber floated down from Doaktown eighty miles away. When the logs jammed the lumberjacks would walk out over the mess and prise and prod till they started moving again. It was a dangerous practice. Many a man who wasn't agile enough lost a leg ... I suppose, listening to these old tales, I became interested in the tree as a living symbol of beauty, not a dead hulk being chivvied along to the paper mills.'

Feeling that they were approaching thin ice, Lindsey

said, 'And Sackville, is it still your home town? I mean, are your family and . . . friends still there?'

'Sure are. I try to make a trip up there whenever I have a fair stretch of free time. There's nothing like a small Canadian town for making you feel at home.'

'With so much warmth there you must have lots of . . . friends?' It was difficult to get over what she wanted to know. 'I mean those that you don't necessarily go salmon fishing with.'

'Like girls, you mean?' He gave a low laugh. 'The ones I grew up with are mostly married. All except Nancy.'

'Nancy?' Lindsey lifted one eyebrow in the dark.

'Nancy Olsen. She lives in the timber house across from ours. She's a couple of years younger than me. When we were kids I used to help her over obstacles on camp trips; carry her books through high school. We went to our first grown-up dance together. Our folks have always considered it a pretty close relationship.'

'You mean like . . . like being engaged?'

'There's an understanding between us.'

Though he worded it differently, Lindsey felt a cold hand close around her heart.

'What's she like?' she asked, instinctively goading herself on to further pain.

'Slim, neat, strawberry-gold hair, likes to dress up.' In pretty pill-box hats and frosted pink suits, Lindsey wanted to say, but the lump in her throat silenced her.

So that was who she had seen him with in Georgetown! Nancy Olsen. His hometown love. A love deep enough, apparently, to bring her all the way from New Brunswick to visit him.

Lindsey felt small and shrunken lying there. So his interest in herself was purely physical. Foolishly, she had assumed all along that the burning attraction which drew them together like a magnet whenever they met was part of a profound and mutually blossoming love. But no. The deep feelings were horribly one-sided. All on her side in fact.

To him she was just a challenge to his male ego, someone he wanted to master as he must have mastered other women in a physical sense. He saw her as an intriguing prospect to add to his string of female conquests, nothing more. The real love of his life was waiting for him in Georgetown.

Fresh tears filled her eyes. Passionate whirlwind affairs were not her style. Not with Brance. So, end of yearning for fulfilment of a love that could never be.

He was telling her about the maple woods in his part of the world, and the maple syrup jamborees they used to have when the sap was boiled over wood fires. Though she felt dead inside she put in a word here and there, asked an occasional question. Then turning with her heartache to the wall she said, 'I think I'll go to sleep now, Brance.'

Through the night, torrential rain thundered around the cabin. It sounded as though the heavens had opened up and even the matted roof of forest greenery above was scant protection for the water which plunged down and could be heard gathering in fast flowing rivulets all around.

When the watery light of dawn filtered through, everything was a damp, depressing mist of dripping greenery and squelching underfoot.

Brance rescued the coffee pot and cooking utensils from around the gutted fire area, and got the stove going inside. For the sake of something to do to offset her leaden feeling, Lindsey reached for ham and eggs from the store shelves and proceeded to fry them over the heat.

While she was thus engaged there was the sound of a vehicle drawing up in the clearing. Brance peered out and told her, 'It's Danny Capucho with my supplies.'

Before she had time to think about anything, the trader had made the dash to the door and was entering, a box of foodstuff in his arms.

'Hi, Danny! Put the stuff over there. You'll have a cup of coffee with us, won't you?' Though the forestry man had spoken naturally enough, Lindsey didn't miss the look of sly bemusement on the Indian's features as his eyes took in the domestic scene of her wielding the frying pan, Brance's demim jacket over her shoulders where he had draped it to ward off the penetrating damp, and the camp table set with everything for breakfast for two.

The owner of the river trading store might be a bushman to all outward appearances, but he was sufficiently civilised to want to bask in the glory of passing on explosive gossip. There would be no need for Brance to say a word of what he had threatened. As soon as Danny got back to the store, the news that the logging boss's daughter had spent the night with Brance Mackenzie in his log cabin, would be all over the district in no time.

Over coffee, the two men chatted about last night's storm. 'At Mazapa Creek, river make much water,' the Indian said. 'Road, no through.'

In his laboured way he was telling them that the road out of the forest was cut off, that they were stranded here until the river went down.

Happier in his native tongue, Brance surprised her by lapsing into the Wapishana dialect for Danny's benefit. For a while she was shut off from their conversation. She had picked up one or two words herself of Wapishana since coming to Guyana, but it wasn't enough to follow what they were talking about, though she did fancy at one stage that some sly reference was made to her presence in the cabin.

After Danny had left, the prospect of being marooned here indefinitely with Brance filled her with dismay and an overwhelming feeling of bleakness. He, on the other hand, was breezy and full of plans. 'The rain will have brought to light several precious plant species which I've been trying to track down,' he said. 'They'll come up like a dream too in this wet. Looks like I'm going to be mighty busy.'

'I'd like to help,' Lindsey offered. It was either that or face a day alone in the cabin with her private misery.

'It's wet,' he warned. 'And uncomfortable.'

'I've lived with the Guyana rains since I was seventeen,' she said tersely. 'I'm probably more hardened to them than you are.'

He gave a grin at this and supplied her with an oversized waterproof hooded cape which would protect her against the drips. He had nothing to offer in the way of footwear, but came up with two stout plastic grocery bags which encased her sandalled feet. These he tied at the ankles with twine.

Catching a glimpse of her reflection in the cabin window she told herself glumly that no way, in this ridiculous get-up, could she compete in his mind with the neat and feminine Nancy.

There was some doubt as to whether the plastic boots had been a good choice when they started out. As she slithered occasionally he asked, without touching her, 'Are you okay?'

'Perfectly,' she replied. If it came to a toss between him steadying her against him or ending up sprawling in the mud, she would choose the latter for her aching heart's sake.

They worked all day in this distant, if companionable, way. Their meals were taken without fuss, round the stove in the cabin. Immediately afterwards they went back to work. By evening the trestle table was groaning with specimens.

When the light failed, Lindsey chose a book from one of a handful on a shelf and schooled her eyes into at least travelling over the print. After a while Brance said, "We'll be running out of kerosene for the lamp. I'd better go to Danny's store to top up. Will you be okay for a while?'

'Of course,' she said without looking up. He didn't return until she was between the blankets feigning sleep.

Three days holed up with Brance in a deserted spot in the forest! How her senses would have reeled at the prospect that first night when they had been locked in each other's arms.

But all that was finished. It had all been just a colossal misunderstanding on her part.

On the third afternoon, when the sun shone and the ground had cleared of rivulets, she didn't bother to tell him she was leaving. Knowing that he had fitted the piece back into the ranch-waggon she simply drove away, and tight-jawed he went on with the jobs he was doing round the open fire.

## CHAPTER SEVEN

DANNY gave her a wave as Lindsey passed by his store. She ignored the implications of his grin, but waved back anyway.

The rain forests were now truly living up to their

name. The green gloom was drenched in a mist oozing moisture. The constant dripping was hardly muscial, but more a twanging on one's nerves; when the earth road disappeared beneath rivers of mud, progress was slow and hazardous. She knew she was taking a chance driving in these conditions, but one more night with Brance would have been too much even for her disillusioned heart to hold out against.

If she had had any doubts as to the speed with which news travelled in the district, these dsiappeared when she arrived back at Springlands.

Apparently rained off from logging, Sam and her father were making the most of the sun on the front porch after the deluge. As soon as she saw them she could tell what was on their minds.

Marching in, she snapped, 'And before either of you say anything, there's nothing at all between Brance and me.'

They quickly lowered their heads over their game of gin rummy and made half-hearted attempts to wipe the satisfied grins off their faces. Exasperatedly, Lindsey stalked off to take a bath.

As the forests dried out, the men went back to work and she was glad of the privacy around the house during the next few days.

She had to devise a plan for seeing Nick. As far as she was concerned nothing had changed regarding their wedding plans, and she hoped he felt the same. Brance had said something about waiting for a cable, to do with what, she didn't know, but if he was hoping to discredit Nick in some way in her father's eyes he was wasting his time. Once she was married, Dad would see that Nick's offer to buy their land and put new life into the Davis Logging Company was by far the best idea.

True, she thought leadenly, she didn't love Nick, but

she loved her father and she was prepared to do anything to save his timber business. Besides, she could devote the rest of her years to building it up into something of an empire for hers and Nick's children. God knew there would be little else to interest her in life.

She dressed carefully in a gingham shirtwaister and placed a white sun hat on her head to add to her demure look.

Driving along the road, she rehearsed in her mind all that she would say to Nick. She would make him understand at the earliest possible moment that the scandal going around was completely unfounded.

When she arrived at the sugar estate the gates were closed. This was not unusual and cheerfully she called out to old Mahdi who attended them, as she had often done in the past. The bent Guyanese was hard of hearing, so she expected to have to wait a little. But when, after calling several times the door of the little hut inside the gate remained pushed to, the pink of a nasty realisation began to creep into her cheeks; especially when she caught a glimpse of Mahdi trying to appear invisible within.

Of course, he was hoping she would save him the embarrassment of having to come out and explain that she was not wanted on Mollenda property.

As she turned away she knew what it felt like to be labelled a scarlet woman. On the drive back to Springlands her face and throat burned with humiliation. She cursed Brance every way she could think of for putting her in this invidious position.

Zina was the only one around the house who expressed no opinions, be it only by looks, on the gossip. At least not until after the following weekend when she returned from her family visit. She touched on it in her dry way then by saying, 'There's a woman asking for your whereabouts in town. Seems riled up about something.'

Lindsey disappeared to her own room before the reason for her crimson cheeks could be misinterpreted. That was all she needed! One of Brance's lady friends, probably going back from the night of the dance, out for her blood. Those Brazilian beauties were noted for their fiery tempers, and how could she explain that she had no designs, less than ever now, on the woman's forestry lover boy?

She swallowed. She was no coward, but she didn't think she would be visiting town for a while.

As time passed, she became more and more convinced that she should search for a way to see Nick. If only she could get a chance to talk to him, to explain . . .

Then one afternoon she had an idea. The far side of the plantation was bounded by the river. She and Nick had often strolled there, leaving their horses to graze. She recalled that once when her horse had strayed she had seen a decrepit footbridge further up the river.

It occurred to her now, that she could drive round to that side of the river and cross over on foot into the cane fields. From there she could easily make her way to Nick's private office.

She dresed much the same as before, knowing that she would definitely need the sun hat this time as protection from the heat during the walk.

The footbridge was grey and splintered with age. It took her weight, but only just. Once across she struck out between the tall rows of sugar cane. She had an uncomfortable feeling of guilt at having to resort to these methods to see her fiancé. Well, as far as she was concerned, the marriage was still on. All she had to do was convince Nick that nothing at all had happened in the log cabin.

An even greater guilt flooded her when she recalled that it might have all been very different if Brance hadn't got the wrong idea about her motives for wanting his lips. But all that was water under the bridge now. She smiled bleakly to herself at the pun. The bridge she had just crossed resembled in many ways the wrecked condition of her emotions these days.

So lost was she in her thoughts, she didn't become aware of voices coming from somewhere within the tall rows of sugar cane until she was almost upon them.

'I'm afraid that's all I can do to help you, Steve.' She froze as she heard Brance's voice drifting through the greenery. 'Pretty soon now I'll have to be moving on. Got a job that's likely to keep me six months or more in Peru. But if you concentrate on breeding, you'll eventually come up with a new hybrid variety resistant to the moth borer pest. In the meantime, step up the fertiliser at the beginning of planting and keep up with the herbicides on the weeds . . .'

His advice to the overseer floated over her. It was the earlier part of his conversation which had sent a cold blast through her heart.

So he would shortly be leaving the district; leaving Guyana. Well, she gulped on a harsh throat, a good job too. Let him go and wreak his damage elsewhere. In the meantime she had to devise a way to put the Davis Logging Company on its feet again.

She bit her lip. The path she was on was wide, more like a dirt road arrowing through the sugar cane. Brance was tall and she was no midget, but she would somehow have to get to Nick's office. It was the only place she knew where she could reach him and where she could explain.

In the end she decided that there was little point in hanging about. It was after all her own affair, and if she hugged the greenery all the way through there was a chance that she could cross the deserted stretch of cane field unnoticed.

Annoyingly, there was a slight rise at the end of the route. Past caring now, she sauntered across the space to the shade of palms where the office stood.

Nick was pacing, a dark look on his face, when she went in. The way it cleared as she entered made her heart leap. Was he actually glad to see her?

'Lindsey!' The manner in which he grabbed her arm and added tersely, 'What are you doing here? You shouldn't have come,' made her all at once uncertain again.

Wasting no time in case he actually had her removed, she poured out the whole story of her imprisonment at the log cabin.

Long before she had finished, she knew that he had no intention of banishing her from his life. There was a feverish eagerness in him at knowing she had come to him, and she had a feeling that he listened with only half an ear to what she said.

'Yes, yes,' he cut her off a little impatiently towards the end. 'But you shouldn't have come here. You know what the atmosphere is like at the moment at the mansion, and if someone should see you with me now . . .'

He was nervous, almost agitated. She was a little disappointed to learn that he was so much under the thumb of the older Mollendas. A person like Nick, polished, almost distinguished-looking apart from a swarthiness about his features, a man of the world, worried as to what his parents might think!

'But we can explain,' she said. 'Tell your folks what

really happened. That it's all a lot of groundless gossip and——'

'Don't you see, it wouldn't work?' From scowling, his face softened momentarily. 'Of course I believe you, darling, but in a situation like that it's going to be very difficult to convince anyone else that you were in Mackenzie's cabin under sufferance.'

Lindsey sighed. 'I see what you mean,' she nodded slowly. 'But what are we going to do?'

'I need time to think.' He put his hands on her shoulders, and she could sense a subdued excitement in him. 'Listen. For now I want you to leave here. You'll find a path on the far side of the palms which leads behind the house and on to the drive. You won't be seen going that way. I'll ring Mahdi to let you out of the main gates.'

Realising that this would mean a long walk back to her car, Lindsey asked with some wonder, 'But aren't you afraid that the gatekeeper will let it out that I've been here?'

'No.' Nick's mouth curled. 'The old man has no source of income other than what I pay him. A word from me and he'll quickly forget having seen you.' He ushered her on her way. 'Don't worry, I'll be in touch with you. But remember, keep out of sight until you're clear of the estate.'

She left with an unpleasant feeling of behaving in an underhand way. She knew all about the pride of some of the Latin races, but this was ridiculous!

The only thing that boosted her morale as she crept off Mollenda property was the knowledge that Nick believed her. That as far as he was concerned, their relationship was on as sound a footing as ever.

She hung about the house waiting in the next few days for news from him. Ben and Sam were curious about her sudden interest in the domestic side of life. Saying nothing, she cooked and sewed and spring-cleaned, content with her secret.

She knew they were seeing Brance on and off at the logging site. They must have wondered why she didn't accompany them occasionally, to take a meal and bed down in the logging camp as she had in the old days. But she was too afraid of missing Nick's message even to worry about keeping up appearances.

Zina viewed her flurry of household activities with her customary impassiveness. Happily, the Negress would continue to pay little attention if Nick was to be daring enough to visit her at Springlands.

Having had this thought, she pulled herself up with wry impatience. All this subterfuge and clandestine goings-on! He might not care to go against his parents' wishes, but she had no such ridiculously outmoded ideas.

Her sole aim where her own father was concerned was to get him to see that the only way to survive as a timber company was to use the money offered for their vast tracts of useless forests, for building it up. And if she had to marry Nick to do it, she was prepared to.

As it happened, the visitor who appeared one afternoon was neither Nick nor anyone else she had remotely expected.

When the car pulled up out on the road she sensed at once that it was a stranger alighting. She guessed that the driver had been instructed to wait. From her chair on the porch she saw him wander off leisurely towards the shade of trees.

She waited, curiously tense, not knowing whether to go out and receive the caller or stay where she was. Seconds later it was doubtful if her surprised legs would have held her, for who should be stepping daintily, if determinedly, up the path than the vision she had seen with Brance in Georgetown. True, the creamy complexion appeared a little jaded in the heat, but the same homely elegance was notable in the neat lime-green linen suit and delicious hat sitting on a tawny gold swathe of hair.

'Good afternoon,' Nancy Olsen greeted her formally as she approached. It was the small, faintly heaving bosom which indicated more turbulent, though admirably suppressed, feelings beneath the green material. 'You haven't been easy to run to earth, Miss Davis,' the voice quivered imperceptibly. 'In my days at the Moratica Hotel I've asked about you, but the townspeople are curiously protective when your name is mentioned. I'm sure I can't imagine why.'

It came to Lindsey then that this must be the woman Zina had mentioned who was on the warpath for her in town. She hadn't known that Nancy was in Moratica. And there she must have caught the full force of the log cabin scandal.

Nancy had no experience of scenes of this sort; the slight dig with which she had ended her opening speech was clearly against her nature. But laudably, she was revolved to put up a fight of sorts for what she considered hers, no matter how much it cost her emotionally.

'I don't believe we've met,' Lindsey said as a means of playing for time.

'No, we haven't met, but I know who you are. And if you know Brance as well as I hear you do, he will certainly have spoken of me.'

The green eyes were startlingly pretty in their ire. Lindsey sensed some slight disappointment there as they lowered to trail over her simple cotton sun-dress, the curtains she was sewing for the living-room windows comfortably bunched on her knee. Perhaps, she mused to herself, her visitor had expected to find a Jezebel type draped on a divan and oozing sex appeal.

'Yes, Nancy, I've heard about you,' she smiled. 'Wouldn't you like to sit down?'

'No, thank you,' came the stilted reply. 'What I have to say, I prefer to say standing.' She drew herself up and added, her tones far from steady, 'I'm leaving for Canada this evening. I simply wanted you to know, before I go, that despite your cheap seduction of Brance, I shall be waiting for him as always when he comes home to Sackville.'

*Her seduction!* Oh, Nancy! Nancy! Where have you been all these years? she wanted to ask. Of course, in your homely little Canadian settlement, far away from the great big world and the men like Brance who drifted around it.

Instead she said quietly, 'Always must have been a long time, Nancy. Brance tells me that you and he grew up together.'

'Meaning that I'm no longer as young as I used to be and that you have the advantage over me there?' The small, pretty nose was pinched.

'No, I wasn't thinking that,' Lindsey shook her head. 'I was wondering . . . well, I mean . . . through school and college together and then dance dates and parties . . .'

'You're wondering why we haven't married before this?' Nancy put the delicate question squarely into words. 'Well, how could I marry with Brance traipsing all over the continent?' Her reply was laced not so much with indignation as evasiveness. 'He's never in one spot for more than six months at a time. How can I cook, clean and sew with a man on the move throughout our life? No. Our home is in Sackville. I've always said I would wait for him there, and that I intend to do.'

'Brance seems steeped in his job,' Lindsey pointed out. 'It could be years before he settles down in one spot.'

'You don't know the tenacity of us Canadian women,' the older woman tilted her head proudly.

But they're not all like you, Nancy. They can't be, Lindsey wanted to say. There must be thousands of the tough northern stock who were willing to accompany their men through endless discomfort, rough living; maybe even in primitive log cabins far removed from neat small-town timber houses sparkling with starched table runners and snow-white doilies.

There was one here who would gladly have gone through the fires of hell just to be at Brance's side through life—if things had been different between them.

Her bruised mind returning to that night at his log cabin, she said evenly, 'I'm sorry we couldn't have been friends, Nancy. If it will make you feel any better on your journey home I'd like you to know that the gossip going round concerning Brance and me is quite without foundation.'

The expression on the mature features was wholly disbelieving, as she had known it would be.

'It will take more than a well-engineered marooning in the forest with the rains as an excuse for you to stay in his log cabin, to come between Brance and me,' Nancy said with a staunch smile.

Obviously limp from the ordeal of having come here to speak her piece, she showed no inclination to prolong the interview. Back and shoulders erect, head high though visibly shaking, she turned to go, saying as she did so, 'I hope we never meet again, Miss Davis. Your kind may do all they can to undermine the loyalties of respectable women, but I can assure you, you haven't succeeded in my case.'

Briskly she departed, taking care not to put a foot wrong on the path, or make a slip which would rob her of her dignity.

After the car had left, Lindsey put the back of her hand against her own hot cheeks. Curiously she was trembling too now, not so much with humiliation as sympathy for Brance. He didn't know it, but the woman he loved was herself in love with the idea of love. If not, why hadn't she married him years ago?

Wasn't it because she was one of those women who occupied themselves with dutifully waiting for the right moment, dreaming of the right moment as a castaway dreams of a good time for leaving the safety of his island, knowing it will never arrive?

She would wait all her life while Brance drifted with his job, and when she was too old, she would accept her spinsterhood, blaming conditions and lapsing into the role of maiden aunt to nephews and nieces as stoically as she had waited for 'the perfect day'.

Lindsey had only met her briefly, but some feminine instinct told her that she was not far out in her appraisal of the genteel Nancy.

However, that was Brance's affair. And who could say, maybe his love for her would prove stronger than that for his job. And with him home for good in Sackville, Nancy might be surprised to find that marriage was inevitable.

She went back to stitching her curtains, but a heavy gloom had settled over her. She wished she could hear from Nick. She supposed it was taking time for him to overcome the old mansion couple's prejudice of her, but this did nothing to ease her impatience. Her own marriage into the Mollenda family was, she felt, the answer to all her troubles. After all, Nick was attractive and he loved her, otherwise he wouldn't have proposed marriage.

Perhaps in years to come she could school herself into feeling something for him. In the meantime, she had the consolation of knowing her relationship with him was something on the same lines as that between Brance and Nancy. She had known Nick since she was seventeen, so why shouldn't it be a natural choice for both of them?

She had overhead Brance say that he would shortly be leaving the district, and she was hoping she wouldn't have to come face to face with him again before he left.

Much to her consternation, he arrived home with Ben and Sam the following evening, and by the look of it all three were in a slightly festive mood.

'We're thinking of having a party,' Ben told her. 'If the weather holds the last tree on Tacana Hill will be cut at the weekend. Brance, here, has fixed up the younger lumberjacks with work with other timber companies. The old-timers that are left, including Sam and myself, are going into the plant export business.' Her father's eyes clouded over as he clapped an arm round the shoulders of the long, lean figure. 'Once he's shown us how to carry on Brance will be leaving us, so we thought we'd deck up the logging camp Saturday night and have a kind of farewell gathering for all concerned.'

'Nice idea,' Lindsey said briefly. 'I'll go and get us all something to drink.'

She needed the excuse to leave the room, for the sight of Brance had undone all her carefully parcelled-up emotions. Her principles were tottering, knowing that he was so close. The hatred she strove to cling to evaporated when she recalled how his lazy gaze had held hers on entering the room.

Trembling, she clattered about in the fridge as though busy routing out iced beers. Really she was playing for time until the old yearnings, the old love, could be suitably suppressed beneath a veneer of calm indifference.

A little woodenly she re-entered the living-room, tray in her hands. The men toasted each other heartily, but she made no move to join in. This wasn't her party, so she took her drink and drifted across the room and out on to the porch.

She knew that beneath his jollity, her father was hurt by her attitude. But she couldn't help herself. Ben might have forgotten that Springlands was historically a proud heritage, but she hadn't. She meant to keep it proud by perpetuating the Davis Logging Company legend her own way.

After a while, though the night was hot and sticky with the ever present threat of rain, her skin rose in goose-pimples. She knew that Brance had joined her on the porch. In the darkness she couldn't see much of him, but her senses were strummingly aware of his nearness.

Trembling again, she wondered how much he knew of her visit to Nick's. Had she, she asked herself worriedly, managed to elude his eye when secretly making her way through the plantation that day?

The answer to these questions was not long in forthcoming.

She heard him place his glass down. He said laconically, 'For a logging woman you seem to be developing a fancy for the rudiments of cane growing these days.'

So he was going to play cat and mouse with her, was he?

'As we're all having to resort to different methods of

making a living round here,' she placed her glass down for a she couldn't trust her shaking hand to hold it, 'sugar cane doesn't seem a bad idea to me.'

'It has its drawbacks, as you probably know.'

She recognised a subtle meaning in his words and answered in like vein, 'Yes, but I'm practised in overcoming drawbacks, as *you* probably know.'

'You mean like sneaking back on to Mollenda property after I've warned you off?'

So it was out now, and blazingly she confronted him. 'Since when has it been your business what I do with my time? Someone ought to remind you that your job is to do with trees, not personal lives.'

'Sometimes they come into my job,' he clipped. 'Yours, for instance, belongs in sticking with your father now that the lumber trade is no longer his life. And if I have to step out of line to get this thing through to you, then too bad!'

'What you're trying to say is, you don't like the idea of me searching for a way to make it up with Nick after you fouled up my character by keeping me at the cabin.'

'What I did, I did for your own good.'

'Like putting a ban on our tree-felling too, I suppose?' she jeered. 'Why not admit it? There are other reasons why you don't want me to patch it up with Nick. Because he's shown what a true friend he is to us in a time of trouble.'

'Sure, he wants to buy your land,' Brance drawled in the darkness.

'Not only that, but the money will set Dad up again in the timber business you destroyed and that will come hard, won't it? Nick playing the benefactor.'

'If you felt something for the guy, I wouldn't give a damn,' he cursed in the shadows.

'Oh, but I do!' She raised her chin. 'I feel I would rather have one good solid neighbour than half a dozen forestry men interfering in a community where they don't belong.'

'That sounds like the perfect basis for renewing your attempts to marry Mollenda,' he sneered.

'I'm willing to supply more than that,' she spoke sultrily. 'Winning Nick over shouldn't be too difficult despite your——'

She had sensed a towering anger building up in him, but she was not prepared for the savage way in which he grabbed her.

'Stay away from Nick Mollenda,' he said between his teeth. The molten fury in his eyes as she struggled pantingly against him unnerved her. She began to see that she might have given away too much of what she was planning in her desire to beat Brance. It had been foolish of her to rise to the bait when he had mentioned Nick, she saw that now.

Rapidly she sought around in her mind for the right words to combat the situation. Keen to put him off the scent as well as to bank down the frightening violence in him, she said, lowering her lashes, 'You needn't worry, your little ruse to create a hotbed of gossip surrounding us both, worked one hundred per cent. True, I did find a back way on to the Mollenda estate to go and see Nick, but he would have nothing to do with me. Neither he nor the senior Mollendas want to see me again.'

Several seconds passed before she lifted her gaze. She had to know if he believed her. She might have guessed that that would be difficult to define; his face was inscrutable. Only his eyes had a sharp glint in them as they raked her features for some confirmation of what she had said.

A smile played at the corner of his mouth; a smile which caused her some unease, but she met his gaze squarely, unflinchingly, and eventually his crippling hold on her slackened.

As it did so she almost crumpled against him. She felt in that pulsating moment before they drew apart that his mouth sought appeasement for his anger. Her own lips yearned to wing their way towards his, but their locked gazes were like a wedge between them.

His smile still there, he let her go and rather than let Ben and Sam know that they had had a scene by rushing through the living-room, she went round and in by way of the front door to her own room.

Tensed more than ever now for Nick's message, Lindsey was glad that the house was still the following afternoon.

When she saw Mahdi shuffling uncertainly on the road near the front of the house, she didn't immediately connect his queer behaviour with anything concerning her. It was only later, as she absently lifted her glance from sewing that her heart leapt. The Guyanese gatekeeper was trying to attract her attention through the bushes growing near the roadside. And he appeared to have something in his hand.

Silently she covered the space from the porch to the spot. Without a word, he pushed a scrap of paper towards her then, turning, fled.

Her fingers shaking slightly she unfolded the note. It was from Nick. He had a plan, he said. There was an old disused sugar mill on derelict land adjoining the Mollenda estate. He wanted her to meet him there at nine o'clock tonight.

Luckily her father planned to spend the night at the logging camp. Just the same, she felt a flicker of irritation. Why was Nick still behaving in this clandestine way? Surely he had spoken to the older Mollendas by now; convinced them that he intended to go ahead with his marriage anyway. Why couldn't he have just invited her to the mansion where they could all talk it out together?

Realising that she could only wait for the appointed hour to sound him out on these points, she bided her time until darkness. When Zina had gone to her own room for the night she climbed into her runabout and stole away as quietly as she could.

Her nerves were considerably on edge on the drive. Remembering Brance's wrath at the mere mention of Nick, she had to admit to feeling a little uncertain now regarding her plans. But then, considering that the forestry man was at the bottom of all this underhand business she was being forced to resort to, an anger of her own propelled her onwards.

But for him, it would have been a straightforward engagement and marriage between her and Nick. It was only because of his penchant for placing obstacles in her way that she was reduced to sneaking out to meet her fiancé in some deserted spot like this.

When she arrived at the derelict sugar-mill she had expected to see Nick's car already there, as it was well after nine. But all was still. She alighted from her own vehicle with some hesitation. It was very dark. The outline of the old mill stood out against the pale wash of night sky like some mediaeval ruin.

She was wondering if she had misinterpreted the note, got the wrong meeting place, when Nick hurried out of the shadows. 'Lindsey! You're late.'

He grabbed her almost accusingly. She had vaguely expected to be greeted with a kiss for her trouble and explained shortly, 'I had to wait until Zina retired. She might have thought it a bit bizarre, me driving off into the night at this hour, and quite frankly I wouldn't have blamed her.'

He quickly softened then. His white, attractive smile apologetic, he said, 'I'm sorry, darling. This business is making us both on edge. It's just that I've waited so long to see you.'

'But why?' Lindsey said in some exasperation. 'Surely it's all straightened out by now? I've explained to you about the log cabin incident. And you say you believe me, so why are we meeting in secret like this?'

'You don't understand,' he said soothingly. 'Of course I believe you, and I want to marry you, but with all the talk that's been going around I can't bring you to the mansion for the moment.'

Recognising that for some reason he was afraid to cross the older Mollendas, she said deflatedly, 'Then what are we going to do?'

'That's why I asked you to meet me here,' he smiled. 'I'm sorry to have kept you waiting, my dear, with no word, but making the necessary arrangements has taken time.'

'What arrangements?' She looked at him closely. 'I don't get it Nick. We were going to get married in the mansion, but now you say the atmosphere being what it is . . .'

'There are other ways of doing as we wish,' his dark eyes held hers. 'For instance we could . . . elope.'

'Elope!' she gasped in the darkness.

'Well, why not?' he replied swiftly. 'The Caribbean Islands aren't far from here. We could fly to Trinidad, go through with the ceremony and be back almost before anyone missed us.'

He hadn't said anything about a honeymoon. Slackly she said, 'Surely the plantation can manage without you for a few days?'

'Of course, but I thought you would be eager to establish our status as man and wife,' he drew her close. 'The gossip has had an unfortunate effect on both our lives. As Mr and Mrs Nicholas Mollenda, we can put an end to it once and for all.'

Lindsey pondered on his suggestion unhappily. She would far rather have seen him overriding his parents' objections because of an old-fashioned distaste for scandal. And she would certainly have preferred to brazen her marriage out under Brance's nose, rather than scurry away for a hole-and-corner affair. And what would her father think?

Hating herself for even considering this kind of deceit, she had to admit that on the other hand the idea did have its advantages. By going away they could avoid the opposition from one quarter and another. And, once they were married, her father would come round to accepting Nick's gracious offer to help them out of their difficulties. After that she could devote the rest of her life to building up the Davis Logging Company. There would be timber again on Springlands one day. In the meantime they could amalgamate with other logging concerns where the forests were workable.

In return for his love, she intended to make Nick a good wife and be a good mother to his children.

Wishing she could feel more zest at having worked it all out so neatly, she said with forced humour, 'Well, what do we do? Just drive off into the blue together?'

'As I say, I've made all the arrangements.' He gripped her eagerly. 'I've got a charter plane standing by at the airfield in Georgetown. We'll have to pick a quiet moment at the plantation. Weekends are best.'

'Dad's arranging a farewell party evening at the Tacana logging camp on Saturday night,' Lindsey said, more to remind herself of the occasion than anything.

'But that would be perfect!' Nick enthused. 'You could go along there so as not to arouse suspicion, then slip away halfway through the evening. I could meet you where the road runs parallel with the river at Potema Creek, at say . . . ten-thirty.'

'All right,' she said dubiously, 'but isn't that a little late for starting out on the long drive to Georgetown?'

'It will be cooler driving at night,' he replied. Then with a brisk look at his watch, 'Darling, I have to go now. But it won't be long before we're together for always. Go back to Springlands now, and don't let anything prevent you from keeping our date. Ten-thirty on Saturday night, remember.' After a brief squeeze he disappeared into the shadows. She realised then that he had made the trip himself on foot from the sugar estate.

She returned to her own runabout somewhat dispiritedly. She could understand Nick not wanting to upset the old Mollendas with what he had in mind, but did they have to be so furtive where everyone else was concerned?

## CHAPTER EIGHT

THE ever-threatening rain was accompanied by rumbles of thunder through the night. Lying sleepless in her bed, Lindsey thought of her father, not yet fully recuperated from his accident. Though he was tough and resilient, his leg bothered him at times, but the loggers' cabins were warm and watertight and he was used to the rough life of the camps.

The rain, when it came, was torrential. It kept Ben

and Sam at the camp all the next day even though they
were rained off from working. Lindsey pictured them
having cosy whisky sessions with Brance round some
stove or other, and instead of feeling radiant at her
forthcoming wedding, she was utterly miserable.

The next day the sun came out. A fresh breeze dried
up the puddles, and to some extent her misgivings. By
Saturday she was once again riding high with her plans
to show Brance that she ran her own life in her own
way.

Ben and Sam were like a couple of schoolboys as they
related to her all the preparations they had been
engaged in for the big night. Many people were coming
from town, they said, including the womenfolk of those
lumberjacks with families locally.

With a poignant catch at her heart, Lindsey
suspected that both these old-timers, so dear to her,
were secretly hoping for a patching up of differences
between her and Brance. She was inclined to believe
also that this was the main excuse for the party, and a
lump in her throat made smiling difficult. If only they
knew that by Sunday, she would be Nick's wife!

She would need a few clothes for her stay on
Trinidad. Smuggling a travelling bag along with her to
the festivities might prove difficult. In the end she
settled for a leather valise, not too bulky, which she
hoped to tuck out of sight in her runabout.

What to wear for the festivities also caused her to
ponder. Her father would expect her to rise to the
occasion in something partyish, yet she couldn't very
well end up at the airfield in Georgetown tomorrow
morning dressed in some evening frippery.

She had a dress whose soft pink material was veined
with a tinselled rose-pink thread, yet its tailored style
made it just about suitable for day as well as evening.

Having settled on that, she proceeded to prepare for her departure, ignoring the tightness inside her. The dress gave her a svelte look, she thought. She had washed her hair. Gleaming, it fell in pale coils on her shoulders. Her skin was perfumed from the bath oils she had used. Though she much preferred her pine soap and bleached safari garb associated with her life as a logging boss's daughter, she felt she owed it to Nick to add these extra touches.

She had an anxious moment when they went out to the cars. She hadn't realised that her father and Sam would automatically assume she would be riding with them. Dressed in serge suits which smelled faintly of mothballs, they waited for her beside the open door of the ranch-waggon like a couple of spruced-up rustic cavaliers.

Her heart missing a beat she said gaily, 'Why don't you two lead the way and I'll follow behind in my runabout.'

Ben's face fell. Obviously proud of his daughter tonight, he wanted the pleasure of showing her off personally when they arrived.

'What do you want a dusty old wreck like that for tonight?' he queried, raising his eyebrows. 'Sam and I have spent all afternoon polishing the ranch-waggon. We planned to do this thing in style.'

'You'll maybe do it in style going,' Lindsey forced herself to sound jocular, 'but what about the ride back? With no telling how much strong drink under your belts you'll be lucky to make the bunks in the nearest cabin at the camp, and I fancy sleeping in my own soft bed tonight.'

The two men grinned at each other sheepishly. Maybe she was right, their looks said. Maybe they wouldn't be steady enough on their feet at the end of the evening to think about making the sedate drive back home.

'I just have to collect a wrap in case it's chilly later,' she said, closing the door on them. 'You go ahead, I won't be far behind.'

Hating herself for the web of lies she was, by necessity, weaving she hurried indoors to retrieve the valise. Outside again, she hid it beneath an old blanket in the back of the runabout.

In the gloom she cast a farewell glance back at the house as she drove away, feeling that she was going to the ends of the earth instead of simply hopping over to a Caribbean island. She wondered what it would feel like to return as Mrs Nicholas Mollenda.

She didn't see anything of the ranch-waggon ahead in the fading light on the drive, nor did she make any attempt to catch up with the two men before they reached the camp. Meeting her father's gaze had been difficult these past two days. The less time she had to spend in his company before ten-thirty, the easier it would be on her nerves.

A glow above the trees towards Tacana Hill indicated the scene where the merry-making was to take place. Other country vehicles were converging from routes along the riverside and soon she was caught in a stream of traffic making for the halo of gold on the hill.

When she arrived at the logging camp she saw that Ben and Sam had good reason to feel proud of their efforts. The clearing was encircled by coloured lights. Not fairy lamps in the true sense of the word, but crude bulbs powered by the camp generator and hastily tipped with whatever paint had been available. The effect was not exactly the height of sophistication, but somehow it gave atmosphere to the surroundings, as did the other additions to the logging camp scene.

There were vats of hot food, pyramids of canned beer and punch bowls for the more genteel drinkers. Felled logs provided the seating arrangements, bran-tubs held surprise packages for the lucky lottery-ticket holders and a group of musicians, practised in performing at rustic functions, played away on a rough timber dais.

Wandering among the gaiety, Lindsey's eyes filled damply when she saw all the little touches that must have cost Sam and her father a considerable amount of work these past days.

But her eyes filled with a different type of tears when a short while later Ben made a speech to open the festivities.

'As you all know,' he told the gathering, 'from tonight the Davis Logging Company and timber business ceases to exist. But we're not sorry that our tree-felling days are over. Brance Mackenzie here has shown us that it's more important to keep our forests for posterity than it is to go hacking them to the ground for fleeting profit.

'He's also taught us that there's a whole lot more to the plant life in our forests than meets the eye. From now on we're going to be proud to be helping the fight against disease by marketing rare specimens for medical science . . .'

As he continued, Lindsey blinked back the angry tears. Her father was wrong. The Davis Logging Company was not dead, not as far as she was concerned. In those moments she almost despised him for accepting defeat so easily. Not so his daughter. Not Lindsey Davis. She had vowed from the start to beat the long lean stranger who had turned their world upside down with his high-handed curtailment of their business freedom. She had resolved to prop up the tottering Davis Company in any way she could after his passing, and in this respect her feelings hadn't changed. All at once she could hardly wait for ten-thirty.

'. . . so don't be downhearted, folks, we're not. We reckon we've got a great future ahead of us and we'd like you all to celebrate with us. Now to start the fun, I reckon nothing could be more fitting than Brance here partnering my daughter, Lindsey, for the first dance of the evening.'

As an ear-splitting cheer went up, Lindsey felt as though all the blood had drained from her at the thought of being enclosed in Brance's arms. She had seen him at a distance, his sky-blue suit sitting well on his lean frame. She had intended to keep things that way. Now as he came forward everyone, including her father and Sam, appeared to be waiting with bated breath for them to merge into each other's arms.

She prayed that her pumping heart wouldn't give her away. Brance's nearness was something she hadn't reckoned on again, ever. How would her body react to his touch? How would her tightly bottled emotions behave in the moment she was drawn against him? Would the stopper fly off, letting free the terrible aching love that she was always having to gather up and stow away in some forgotten corner of her heart?

Luckily, Brance was relaxed, and she did her best not to appear wooden in his arms. They did a round of the beaten earth space to the added cheers of the onlookers.

Once a flood of other couples took to the floor, Lindsey thought the strain would have eased. On the contrary, it only increased as they were jostled against one another by the waltzing throng.

Brance's closeness affected her to the very marrow of her bones. Steeling herself not to run from him, she said tightly, 'Do we have to continue with this farce?'

'If we don't want to upset Ben,' his grin masked a

stony determination. 'And I don't think you're selfish enough to spoil his night, despite that headstrong defiance of yours.'

'My father's ideas are not my ideas,' she muttered.

'Well for the moment they're going to have to be,' he pepped up their dancing. 'Everyone believes that log cabin saga, remember, so why don't we give the folks a run for their money?' His good humour taking over, he whirled her between the other couples.

She did try, remembering the look in her father's eyes, to enter into the spirit of the thing; but how could she tell her heart, her physical being that this was only a game, just a sham romance of the moment, not the love of a lifetime that she and her heart cried out for?

She realised with a sudden chill that Brance was watching her closely. 'I'd get more reaction dancing with one of the timber seating logs,' he quipped. 'Yet I could swear I had a warm and lovely girl in my arms.'

His piercing enquiry was the last thing she wanted right now, but before she could avert her gaze he crooked an eyebrow down at her. 'Something doesn't fit,' he said. 'It's not like you not to have a little fight in you at a time like this.'

Every part of her keyed up ready for her flight later on, it was all she could do to keep herself from shaking. 'You may be able to live down the pretty gossip you started,' she clutched at any excuse and poured ice-water into her voice, 'but I don't have your thick, armadillo hide.'

'You can acquire anything with practice,' he shrugged. 'Now, if you were to mould yourself against me and we sort of got to dancing cheek to cheek I bet we could fool everyone at this gathering into thinking——'

'No! Let me go!' She ought to keep the hysteria out

of her voice, but afraid she had allowed her nerves to get the better of her she hurriedly added, 'Brance, I'm just not in the mood for dancing at the moment. Don't forget this is everybody's big night except mine.'

'How could I?' He twisted a grin. 'Still carrying a torch for the Davis Logging Company? Or for that female cussedness that won't let you forget the war is over?'

'I said I wanted to be left alone!' She broke free of him at the edge of the dancers, bethinking herself to add stiltedly, 'I'd really rather just enjoy the evening with my friends, if you don't mind.'

'Okay! Okay!' He spoke with tolerant humour while eyeing her with a queer look. 'If I know Ben, he and Sam and some of the older loggers will have taken off to one of the cabins to enjoy the party in their own way. So ... if that's what you want,' he gave her a farewell salute, 'have fun.'

Limp with tension, she almost collapsed when he left her, but the carefree atmosphere helped to knit together her mangled nerves. Soon she found she could stroll and chat with people she knew from town, share a joke with the lumberjacks and their wives or girlfriends, in a reasonably calm way.

She did everything to give the appearance of having as good a time as anyone else. She ate a dish of the tasty food while chatting brightly to Bob Lasley, the camp cook. She drank a cup of punch, listening to innumerable toasts from one noisy group or another, and showed as much excitement as to whether her lottery-ticket would be one of the lucky numbers as the other members of the gathering.

Brance didn't bother her again. She saw him from time to time through the evening, drinking and joking among the timber men, and joining in the various card games, always a popular sport in a logging camp and one that her father and Sam would no doubt be indulging in by this time.

Just as there were loggers' cabins given over to the men for their entertainment, so there were others where the women could gossip among themselves, discuss cake recipes and generally enjoy female companionship.

Lindsey was glad of this. Drifting towards one of these cabins would take her close to where she had left her runabout in the shadows. After spending a short time in the interior no one would miss her in the comings and goings of the womenfolk.

Glancing at her watch, she saw with accelerating heartbeats that it was already aften ten. The spot where she was to rendezvous with Nick was quite a few miles from here.

She allowed herself only a few minutes where hair was being crimped into place and skirts straightened, then, as though making back towards the music, she struck out instead into the darkness.

It was a tedious business picking her way over the rutted ground to her transport. Her heart hammering now, every whoop of laughter or raised voice near by riveted her. Feeling foolish, Lindsey told herself that even if anyone came upon her she could be simply preparing to drive home, couldn't she? Not everyone wanted to stay till the early hours making merry in the outdoors.

Just the same, she moved off silently. Once she had put a reasonable distance between her and the homely fires and bright lights of the camp, she should have been able to relax. It was just the fleeting vision of her father's happy face back there which unsteadied her at the wheel.

But everything would soon be all right, she told

herself. He would accept Nick for a son-in-law if he knew it was what she wanted. And he would see then that there was little point in refusing Nick's offer to take the useless forest stretches off their hands.

With renewed spirit, she gave herself to the business of driving. The roads hereabouts were riddled with obstacles. Pot-holes lay in wait for the unwary eye, and, hypnotised in the glare of the headlights, forest animals would leap across at the last split-second, making one swerve and grit one's teeth.

Catching a ghostly glimpse of herself in the mottled rear-view mirror, she smiled wryly at her elegant get-up. Hardly the attire in which to be bouncing and bumping through the night in a dusty old runabout! But once she was in Nick's sleek shooting brake heading for the coast, her clothes would be more in keeping with the occasion.

Gripping the wheel, she reckoned that by this time she had covered half the journey to Potema junction. A glance at her watch told her that she would easily make the meeting place for ten-thirty.

She was congratulating herself on the smooth way she had made her exit from the logging camp gathering when a tiny glow of light caught her eye in the mirror. A vehicle some way behind her, obviously. Someone else leaving the festivities? Probably.

She gave her attention to the route and prepared herself for the momentous meeting with Nick.

The beaten earth track wound this way and that. She branched off after a while on the lonely route that would take her to Potema Creek. Nick had chosen their rendezvous spot cleverly, she realised. There wouldn't be a soul along that stretch of river at this time of night.

Time on her side, she was ambling along—until she caught sight of the light, still way back in the gloom in the rear-view mirror. Strange! No one else would have cause to drive to a forsaken spot like the creek at this hour.

For the first time since starting out she felt a flicker of apprehension. She was ready to swear that those lights, the headlights of another conveyance, were the same ones which had been behind her way back on the forest road. But why would they have turned off along the lonely creek route? Unless ... her mouth went suddenly dry ... *unless they were trailing her.*

She rallied from the shock of this possible setback to clamp her foot on the accelerator. Well, there was one certain way to find out. And with only a short way to go to the creek, whoever it was nosing into what didn't concern them would quickly regret their curiosity.

From then on she literally shot through the night. Forest life had to take care of itself, and the riverside community of birds squawked in indignation at her passing. But driving at such break-neck speed became extremely hazardous in the old runabout. And while she gritted her teeth and rattled around the inside, Lindsey saw that the headlights behind her had indeed taken up the chase, as she had more or less suspected they would. Not just that, but by now they were gaining on her at an alarming rate.

She cursed the ancient logging vehicle which had always stood her in good stead for normal use, but was no match for the nimble, speedy movements of the other thing on the track. It hopped around like a sprightly firefly, while her own efforts to outpace it were like those of a stricken glow-worm.

And soon she saw why. As the space rapidly narrowed between them it became clear that the headlights hounding her with such smooth, if erratic, precision belonged to nothing less than a sturdy jeep. *A jeep!* Her heart shot into her throat. There was only one man around here who owned a jeep. *Brance!*

Hot resentment flooded in, after the initial jolt of knowing he was behind her had subsided. How dare he take it upon himself to shadow her through the night like this! Who did he think he was, staying hot on her tail when she had given more than enough hint that she wished to proceed unhampered?

Only a few minutes away, Nick would be waiting for her. They would waste no time on her arrival at Potema Creek, but would streak away to Georgetown in his powerful shooting brake. And anyway they had been reduced to this kind of underhand get-away by the man who had the nerve now to pursue her unswervingly.

Furiously she urged the runabout to go faster. The jeep leapt almost on to her bumper. It hung on as she slewed this way and that, then at a widening of the track it shot up alongside her, remaining there leech-like so it was all she could do not to burst into tears at his tenacity.

She didn't, of course. Fury giving her strength, she kept up her bone-jarring speed. Nose to nose the two vehicles bumped through the night. Then, deftly choosing his moment, Brance took the jeep forward.

He drove ahead at a far greater speed than she could ever hope to attain, and some distance clear of her, jumped on his brakes so that the jeep slewed, making an effective barrier across her path.

Throwing on her own brakes, Lindsey almost fell out of her seat in her vexation. 'Perhaps you wouldn't mind telling me why you have to pick a darkened forest track to indulge in your childish Grand Prix aspirations?' she flared acidly.

He extricated his long legs from the jeep and in the glow of the headlights strolled over. 'Why the hurry?' he drawled, ignoring her murderous mood.

'If there are any questions to be asked,' she countered quiveringly, 'it should be me enquiring what right you think you have to tail me through the night as though I wasn't perfectly free to drive where I please?'

He shrugged and replied leisurely, 'You've been acting mighty strange all evening. I took to wondering why you were so on edge about everything. When I saw you slope off, I figure that it might have something to do with why you'd been going round the party chatting and smiling with everyone and looking as though you were going to fall apart.'

'I don't suppose it's occurred to you,' she seethed, 'that they're my father's celebrations, not mine. I don't fête the loss of a business. I do something about hanging on to what we've got.'

'Sure, you've always been a spirited logging filly,' he eyed her closely. 'But what, I ask myself, are you up to this time?'

'Do I have to be up to something?' she laughed hollowly, afraid that she might have given too much away in her outburst. 'Is there any reason for suspicion simply because I make an early exit from what I don't consider concerns me?'

'An exit to where, Lindsey?' His gaze narrowed. 'This is not the way back to Springlands, and we both know it.'

'Couldn't I be out just driving for the air?' Her voice quaked, for she knew that her suggestion bordered on the ridiculous.

As though in agreement he sloped a mirthless grin. 'I hardly think so, when you practically fled up a wallaba to avoid me catching up with you.'

She realised she was trapped as far as excuses for being where she was, on the way to Potema Creek, were concerned. And in her nervousness she flicked a glance to the interior of the runabout to make sure her travelling valise was well hidden. It was, and would probably have remained so but for this careless slip on her part.

'This is wild country.' As though to give credence to his words he inclined an ear to the sound of forest night life, glanced about him at the thick jungle-like undergrowth, the sinuous stretch of river just visible in the star glow through the trees. 'Nobody comes this way at this time of night.' His gaze took to raking her again. 'Leastwise, not unless they're expecting someone else to turn up at a given spot.'

With that, he reached into the runabout and flicked aside the blanket.

## CHAPTER NINE

BRANCE was not one given to displaying his emotions, but she saw his jaw harden in an odd way as he fished out the valise. 'Going away?' he said almost lightly, flicking it open and examining the contents.

Colouring as some of her more intimate garments were displayed in the brash glare of the headlights, Lindsey said coldly, 'Do you mind?'

He snapped the valise shut and tossed it back where he had found it. 'Looks like I interrupted something,' he smiled dangerously. 'You *are* on your way to a given spot, and I don't need three guesses as to who's going to be waiting for you when you get there.'

'All right. Yes, I'm on my way to meet Nick,' she flung at him, the strain and tension of the evening all at once proving too much for her nerves. 'If you must know we're driving to Georgetown tonight. Tomorrow we shall be boarding a plane to Trinidad, where our wedding ceremony—temporarily hindered from taking place at the mansion by your log-cabin tactics—will go ahead as planned.'

'I see.' In the beam of the headlights, his features appeared to be hewn out of copper; with the exception of his mouth which sloped queerly. 'And you're doing all this because you can't bear to be parted another moment from lover-boy Mollenda.'

'I happen to be very fond of Nick,' she lied.

He shrugged. 'I can't say I admire your tastes. But I reckon we both know they're coloured slightly by the fact that Nick's offered to take your land off your hands.'

'And what if they are?' She tossed her head. 'Business marriages often turn out more successful than those entered into supposedly for love.'

She was breathing rapidly, her emotions in shreds. It was aggravating to see Brance as cool as always.

'You've got all the answers, haven't you, Lindsey?' Though his eyes were narrowed, he smiled. 'You really mean to go down fighting, true to the old traditions of the die-hard logging woman.'

'I intend to marry Nick, if that's what you mean,' she spoke shakily while forcing her own lips to smile. 'And there's nothing you can do to stop me. I'm old enough to make up my own mind.'

'That's right,' he nodded. His calm stance unsettled her. It wasn't like Brance to stand by when she had the upper hand in an argument.

Jerkily she said, 'Now if you don't mind I'll continue my journey. I'm expected at Potema Creek, less than a quarter of a mile away round the next bend. And if you don't want to get your jeep crumpled I suggest you move it, because I won't let it stop me going to Nick.'

She wasn't bluffing. She had weighed up the position in the headlights and she reckoned she could scrape by without hitting the trees.

Coasting along on the exhilaration of having won for once, she got behind the wheel of the runabout and started up.

Brance watched her. 'You're right,' he said folding his arms. 'I wouldn't want to stop you suiting yourself. And I guess the jeep's no deterrent for that pig head of yours.'

She didn't want to listen to any more. Tears were threatening, though why they should be when she had won, was crazy.

'You want to marry Nick, right?' He raised his voice above the engine as she started off.

'Right,' she flung back aiming for the space between the track and the trees.

'And you want to sell him the land that my organisation has stopped the Davis Logging Company from cashing in on the timber. Right?'

'Right,' she yelled defiantly, hearing the tearing of metal as a greenheart declined to step aside at her passing. But she was through. She was on her way.

'Even though,' his voice followed her as she went, 'it's worth several million times more than Nick's price, or anything you'd get for the timber?'

She had been about to get up speed. While she sat suspended in this peculiar vacuum, her foot poised on the accelerator, Brance called, 'No, it's not the racket of that old steam engine playing tricks on your ears, Lindsey. You heard correctly. That stretch of Springlands forests is worth several million times more than the price Nick's offering your father.'

She gripped the wheel, undecided what to do. She had been so sure that she had turned the tables at last on Brance's supremacy where their logging business was concerned. But now she was remembering Nick's peculiar behaviour lately.

Trembling, she twisted in her seat and asked, towards where Brance was standing in the headlights of the jeep, 'Who says so?'

'This.' He took a piece of paper from his pocket and waved it. 'It's the cable I've been waiting for. It confirms my hunch of why Mollenda has been so keen to get his hot little hands on those forests. There's enough bauxite there to make the mining town of Mackenzie look like a children's sand pit.'

Lindsey slumped. It wasn't true! It couldn't be. Surely Nick wouldn't be so ruthless as to cheat her father while pretending to help him.

Brance came towards her slowly. He opened the door of the runabout and took her hand. 'You'd better come and sit in the jeep, Lindsey,' he said gently. 'There's a lot more you'll have to hear, I'm afraid.'

When she was seated beside him he began. 'It seems Mollenda's had his eyes on those forests for several months. From what I discovered in Georgetown, he's a past master at buying apparently worthless land and then cashing in on its potential. Unbeknown to Ben—or you—he's had a geologist's report on the soil content in that area within the last few weeks. Natually, when he discovered what he was on to, he's wasted no time in arranging the whole deal.

'There's a processing firm based in New York, all set to begin the mining. That's what's taken the time. A company on to something as big as this doesn't give away that kind of information easily. But I've got friends who specialise in worming out the unsavoury. And as I suspected the man behind the deal is one Nicholas Mollenda, residing in Guyana.'

'I can't believe it,' was all Lindsey could say faintly. But couldn't she? Hadn't she been vaguely aware from the beginning that Nick's behaviour towards her had been odd? Hadn't it struck her that his romantic overtures were rather sudden?

As though reading her mind, Brance said, 'Mollenda offered your father a price for the land. But he was shrewd enough to know that Ben was sentimentally attached to Springlands as a whole, so he covered himself against a no-sale by quickly sweeping you off your feet. Married into the family, he reckoned he'd soon be controlling the bauxite treasure anyway.'

Lindsey shook her head slowly to clear away the mists of her bewilderment. 'My father has known Nick since he was a boy of fifteen,' she whispered, white-faced. 'It's incredible to think that he hoped to cheat him so calmly.'

'It doesn't come difficult to Mollenda,' Brance said grimly. 'And at the moment he's a pretty desperate man. People who are owed money don't mind voicing their complaints, and I met plenty in Georgetown with a grudge against our Portuguese dandy. He's used to the rich life, but apparently profits from his land piracy have not been sufficient of late to cover his gambling debts. He's in so deep he's mortgaged half the sugar estates. So you can see, he badly needs to get his hands on that bauxite. It's the answer to all his troubles, to say nothing of providing him with gambling fodder for the rest of his life.'

Lindsey went cold now when she recalled Nick's nervousness the afternoon she had sneaked in to see him in his plantation office. That would explain why he had a terrible dread of upsetting the senior Mollendas. If he had shown scant regard for their opinions by insisting that the wedding in the mansion proceed as planned, the whole sorry story of his embezzlement of family funds might have come to light in the upset. And this was something he was not prepared to risk.

Staring down at her hands in her lap she asked, 'Have . . . you known all this for some time, Brance?'

'Ever since I went to Georgetown,' he shrugged. 'But I couldn't prove anything about Mollenda's interest in your land until I received the information from New York.'

'Does Dad know . . . all these things about Nick?' she forced herself to query, her gaze still lowered.

'No. I thought it better to keep them to myself pending further enlightenment.'

At this reply, she almost smiled to herself in a broken way. Her father had always got along with Nick, and he had known nothing to alter his feelings in this direction. Yet he had shown no great emotion at her possible marriage to their neighbour. Why? Was it, as she had once suspected, that Nick was one of those men who fostered an instinctive caution in other males?

'If he's so short of ready cash,' she asked puzzled, 'how come he could make us an offer for the forests?'

'The mining firm was putting up the money,' came the dry answer.' He was staking everything he had on pulling the deal off.'

And the fact that he had almost achieved his aims, made her blood run cold.

'What about the bauxite?' she asked then. 'Have you told Dad the news?'

Brance replied in the negative. 'I only picked up the cable this afternoon,' he added. 'With all the merrymaking going on there hasn't been time to get him on his own.'

Recalling her father's glowing countenance amid the logging camp festivities she voiced a dread in low tones,

'He doesn't know that I walked out on his party to . . . to . . .'

'I doubt it,' Brance grinned reassuringly. 'I left him enjoying a winning streak at poker, and with a red-hot hand to play.' He added then with closed expression, 'If we get back now, he'll never know.'

Lindsey's watery smile was sceptical. 'How am I going to explain a badly chewed-up fender on the runabout?' she asked remembering the agonised crunch of metal as she had tried to clear the trees.

'We'll leave it here,' Brance shrugged. 'I'll have it picked up tomorrow and worked on. It's a jalopy anyway, he won't notice a quick repair job.'

He climbed out to go and manoeuvre the runabout to the side of the track and switch off the headlights. Lindsey stared past him to the route beyond where, if it had been left to her determination, she would now be speeding along to her destination. What had seemed only minutes before the answer to everything, was now like a hideous dream.

Nick had been planning to deceive and swindle her father long before Brance had come on the scene. And she had been rushing into his arms, unknowingly furthering his ends. Of course an elopement would suit Nick perfectly! A quick wedding ceremony, then, once he was sure that the bulk of the proceeds from the bauxite was coming his way, their marriage would no doubt mean less than nothing to him.

Aware that the lean, shadowy shape had returned to slide in behind the wheel, she said in choked tones, 'Take me back, Brance. Take me as far away from Potema Creek as possible.'

On the drive through the darkness, she was struck by the irony of her distaste for Nick's methods. Hadn't she had an ulterior motive too for wanting to marry him?

But she had been prepared to give her life as a wife to him to make up for this small deceit.

Bitterly, she realised now she could have expected nothing as generous from Nick. She supposed she had always known he was cold and ruthless at heart, but she had willed herself to overlook these traits in her wild desire to triumph over Brance.

Yet it was Brance who had caught her back from the edge of the precipice tonight.

She had been poised to wed Nick; intent on coaxing her father into selling him the land, not knowing that they would have been handing over a fortune.

But Brance had checked her in time. She had him to thank for not having to meet the look in her father's eyes when he discovered the truth.

The logging camp festivities were in full swing when they returned. The cabins of diverse entertainments werre now being deserted for the cheery glow of fires where hot dogs and other tasty snacks were being prepared.

The musicians, fresh from a break and refreshments, were playing livelier than ever.

Lindsey was dancing with Brance when her father took to circulating anew among his guests. Though she moved mechanically, she found the taut frame instilling her with the strength to carry on as though nothing had happened.

Still in a state of shock at what might have taken place, it was only due to Brance's encouragement that she got through the rest of the evening at all.

The riotous barn-dancing, the competition for the best contestant at shovel-board, the race without spilling a drop of punch, she joined in all the fun because Brance was there, his grin inspiring her with the confidence to smile over her self-inflicted anguish.

When she drew a sugar-pig in the lottery and he a perfumed sachet they laughed uproariously, and nobody knew the real reason for the tears in her eyes.

Ben and Sam viewed daughter's and the forestry man's togetherness with sly, conspiratorial smiles on their rosy faces. Their crowning satisfaction came towards the end of the evening when Brance bade everybody good night and drove Lindsey away in his jeep.

The trip back to Springlands was made in silence. Lindsey felt utterly spent after the ordeal of putting on a gay front. She had behaved recklessly and foolishly tonight, she knew that now. But the admittance did little to relieve her depressed state.

There were pink spots of colour in her pale cheeks. Her hair gusted back from her face like strands of wild silk in the breeze. She breathed in the damp, dark night and wished she could wash herself clean from the ugliness of deceit and rashness.

When they finally drew in beneath the tall trees that screened the house she had recovered fractionally from her apathy to step unaided from the jeep. In the same numb way she made for the porch. She hadn't realised that the tall lean figure hovered at her side with a steadying hand at the ready until she turned in the porch to wave good night and almost collided with him.

'Good night, Lindsey,' he said in reply to her whispered one.

'Oh, and Brance,' her hand on the knob she paused, as he was about to move off. 'Thank you for what you did tonight.'

'All in the line of a forestry man's duty.' There was the ghost of the old mockery in his eyes as he took his leave of her with a lazy salute.

\* \* \*

The cicadas' call sounded metallic on the rain-charged air. A jewel beetle plodded on its way past the steps of the porch. Over by the road, butterflies with iridescent wings were like blue lights bobbing among the hedge of oleanders.

Several days had passed since the logging camp gathering. Ben had been little moved at the news that there was bauxite on his land; he decided he liked the forests as they were. He was more excited at the way the Davis plant export business was rapidly coming into being.

The Mazapa saw-mill was being converted into a processing factory. There would be a raw material section right through to a classified container room, plus loading bays, delivery department and despatch office.

Orders were already coming in, proving that his plants were in great demand not only in the medical field, but also for cosmetic and culinary purposes. It looked as though a sizeable work-force would be needed, and this cheered Ben no end. Maybe he couldn't keep on the bulk of his loggers, but those who had womenfolk would be assured of a job gathering the plants.

And now that he was on his way, Brance was packed ready to leave. He had dropped in at Springlands to say goodbye, and the afternoon had been spent in idle chat out on the porch, where the air was less sticky, plus one or two last-minute queries that Ben wanted to put concerning the new plant business.

'What's the position,' he asked now as Lindsey topped up the men's drinks then returned to her chair under the window, 'if we wanted to process the plants right through to the drugs stage?'

'You'd need a lot of expensive equipment for that,'

Brance informed him. 'But there's nothing complicated in the operation. In a couple of years you might feel disposed to add laboratories and such.'

Ben shot him a half-amused look, then as he sounded him out, 'Tell me, Brance, did you have some sort of wind that I shouldn't let go of that land? Is that why you suggested starting up in plants?'

Brance smiled, but gave no direct answer. 'In our job,' he said, 'we're expected to turn up something, where we can, to compensate for any hardship caused. In mentioning that you'd probably make as much cashing in on your rare plant specimens as you had been doing from timber, I was simply performing my duty.'

Ben appeared content with this before a worried look flickered across his countenance. 'Supposing the government forces me to open up a bauxite mine, saying it's vital to the economy?'

'They're not likely to as it's your land. But if they did, we'd just remind them that they made a deal with us to preserve those forests.'

Ben breathed again. 'You know something,' he smiled into space,' I reckon those hardwoods are pretty majestic giants to think about slicing with a saw.' And with a glance her way, 'Are you with me, Lindy?'

'Have been for some time,' she smiled truthfully. 'There's something almost sacrilegious about ploughing flourishing trees to the ground.'

'And you, Sam?'

His stubbly-chinned chief logger shrugged happily and put it in his own words. 'It's going to be a darn sight easier moving plants than it was tussling with them mangy greenheart brutes,' he said with a tobacco-stained grin.

Brance got to his feet. 'Time I was leaving,' he said. 'Got to get to Georgetown by tonight. First thing tomorrow my plane takes off for Peru.'

He shook hands with Ben. Their grip lingered a long moment, and with considerable male affection their glances held. Then, slapping him on the back Ben joked, 'Don't go upsetting those Peruvians. They're mustard if things don't suit, and we want to see you around here again one day.'

After Sam had said his goodbyes in his warm awkward way, the two old-timers, exchanging anxious, twinkling glances, began to shuffle towards the indoors.

'There's no need to go in, you two.' On her feet, Lindsey smiled over her discomfort. She knew what was behind their surreptitious movements, and her heart ached for them. 'I'll just walk Brance to the jeep,' she said lightly, 'then we'll wave him off together.'

She was making it clear, of course, to save Brance embarrassment, that there was no reason for her and him to be left alone. Contrary to her father's and Sam's hopes, they had nothing to say to each other in these last moments.

Brance was preparing to move on to fresh parts, and he would always have Nancy Olsen waiting for him in Sackville. He didn't know that Lindsey had seen him with his home-town love in Georgetown. And Nancy certainly wouldn't have told him that she had made the trip to Springlands to have it out with the 'scarlet woman'.

No, she had nothing to say to Brance, though her heart was overflowing with love and the pain of containing it almost more than she could bear.

Forcing a sparkle of sorts to hide the dry, unshed tears in her eyes, she kissed him gaily on the cheek and said for all to hear, 'Goodbye, Brance. Despite our tiffs in the past, I want you to know that I think you're the tops in forestry men.'

'So long, Lindsey.' There was irony in his gaze and something else, then he was draping himself behind the wheel and starting up the engine.

He shot away, looking back only to give a last wave towards the porch. Seconds later he was gone, the sound of his jeep echoing noisily as he tore off along the road.

When Lindsey turned it seemed to her that the two men standing on the porch had aged in some tear-blurred, touching way. Two bent, disconsolate figures, they made the weight of her grief doubly difficult to bear.

They didn't know about Nancy Olsen. They didn't know that Brance carried his dream of the perfect woman back in Sackville, around in his heart. And what was the point of telling them?

'Well, for heaven's sake!' she said, marching up the steps. 'Do we have to be so funeral-like about everything? People come and go.'

She fled to her room then, before her bright acceptance of things shattered leaving the shell of a woman that had once been bold, spirited Lindsey Davis.


From her chair in the living-room she watched how the birds swooped past the windows on the unsettled air. There were still a few hours of daylight left on this Saturday afternoon. Trudging off with their disappointment Ben and Sam had gone to the saw-mill. They planned to fish in the creek there and camp till Monday morning.

She supposed she ought to have discouraged them with heavy rain threatening. But she could find no words with which to bridge the hurt silence of their disappointment, and they had stowed their gear in the ranch-waggon and driven off.

She had the house to herself. She was seized with a mild panic at the thought of somehow getting through the rest of the day. A few hours had become terrifying to contemplate. *What was it going to be like getting through the years?*

She schooled herself into staying sane. The memory of Brance would fade with time. She would fill her life with work, with plans; she would make the Davis horticultural enterprise the biggest thing in South America. She laughed almost hysterically, because the tears were in danger of blinding her.

It seemed that her every heartbeat clocked off the distance that was ever growing between her and the man she loved more than anything in the world.

Slackly, she decided to make a start at coming to terms with this new, dark section of her life by putting the kettle on for a cup of tea.

She had risen from the chair when a sound outside caught her attention. She wasn't expecting visitors. She started towards the front window to see who had arrived. Before she could reach it a figure had darkened the living room doorway.

'Nick!' she gasped. 'What on earth are you doing here?'

It wasn't just his sudden presence that startled her. His appearance was not in keeping with his usual groomed air. His cream riding breeches were dusty and crumpled. His silk shirt opened haphazardly at the front showed a wedge of chest covered with dark fuzz.

'You and I are going to make a little trip.' His smile was far from attractive now. There was something wild about it, and the look in his eyes.

Her insides tightening, she realised that he knew she was alone in the house. He must have bided his time close by, watching and waiting for a moment such as this.

Speaking strongly over an inexplicable fear which gripped her, she said, 'I'm not going anywhere with you, Nick. Not after the way you tried to cheat my father.'

'It wasn't very polite of you not to turn up at Potema Creek as we arranged,' he murmured, ignoring her comment. 'You wanted me, and you wanted my money to save Ben's neck. Well, once you make a deal with Nick Mollenda you don't back out, Lindsey.'

She gave a hollow laugh and wished she hadn't, for blades of annoyance flashed in his eyes. 'Your money! Nick, I know you're in trouble up to the hilt and that you were relying on the bauxite to get you out of the financial mess you're in.'

'I still am,' he said smoothly. 'You see, although Ben knows about the bauxite now, the situation between us two is still the same. You and I planned to become joined in union. Because you have had a slight change of mind about furthering your own ends, it doesn't alter our arrangement—I still plan to further mine.'

'You must be out of your mind,' Lindsey could not help but scoff. 'You surely don't think I'd go ahead with our wedding plans after the bare-faced way you tried to rob us?'

'Who said anything about a wedding?' he shrugged. And then with an offhand smile, 'Later perhaps, when it becomes, er . . . necessary.'

She felt a chill like icy fingers trailing down her spine, though she was not quite sure what he meant by this.

Obligingly he went on, 'What I had in mind was an elopement of sorts . . . a romantic interlude, shall we say, in some secluded spot. Ben is a staunch family man as we both know, he has always wanted to do the best for you. I'm sure when he knows that he has, er . . . a grandson on the way, he'll be keen to name him, along with you, as legatee of all that bauxite wealth. And as I will have fathered the precious Davis heir, it's hardly likely that I'll be left out in the cold, so to speak.'

Lindsey couldn't believe her ears. She had at one time resigned herself to having Nick's children, but looking at him now she wondered how in heaven she could ever have contemplated the idea. As a man he repelled her.

'You underestimate my father,' she said trying to keep the quake out of her voice, 'if you think he would calmly accept a marriage by force.'

'But would it be, *meu bonita*?' His Portuguese ancestry came out in his caressing tones. 'We were to be betrothed, were we not? And Ben is anxious for a son-in-law and grandchildren. In the old days when I gave a hint of my intentions he did not seem too averse to the idea. And you are a young, warm-blooded and perhaps lonely woman now that Mackenzie has left the district. I'm sure your father would understand your, er, . . . need for me under the circumstances.'

Lindsey trembled outwardly now. Though much of his argument was the product of an unbalanced mind, there was just a chance that he could reap some dubious gain from his threat.

'You're despicable!' She forced herself to keep the fear out of her voice. 'But of course, I've always known it. If I'd obeyed my instincts instead of fooling myself into believing that you were a genuine friend to Dad and me, I would never have let you put a ring on my finger.'

He glanced briefly at her hand, bereft now of the jewel, and shrugged. 'Trinkets are now of little consequence. It is the sealing of our . . .' his cruel mouth sloped, 'affection which will join us far more securely in the end.'

Her legs shaking beneath her, she sensed that he was becoming weary with talk.

'My father and Sam will be returning at any moment,' she bluffed. 'They were only driving as far as the river to check on the flood level.'

Nick gave her an unhinged smile. 'I happen to know that they loaded camping gear and sleeping bags,' he said with merciless amusement. 'Seems to me they expect to be gone overnight.'

So he had been near enough to the house to watch that kind of goings-on. There was something macabre in picturing him lying in wait outside Springlands.

Her terror almost choking her, she made a feeble attempt to play for time. 'Look, Nick,' she said brightly, 'why don't we talk this thing out? Why don't the three of us have a rational discussion? I'm sure we'll come to some solution regarding your money problems. I promise you that when my father returns I'll send for you, and I'll do all I can to persuade him to help you.'

'You backed down on a promise once before, Lindsey,' he advanced smiling. 'I don't intend to have my plans upset by your change of heart a second time.'

Wildly, Lindsey searched her mind for what to do next. His path towards her blocked the way to the outdoors. Thinking only that she couldn't bear him to touch her, she made a dash for the hallway that led to the kitchen.

It was not the cleverest of moves for his strides ate up the distance in seconds. But she had the advantage of knowing every facet of the house's structure and furnishings.

While he was stumbling in the poor light against a wall-side table which disguised a jutting beam, she had reached the kitchen and slammed the door after her. But what kitchen door has a key! The one at Springlands didn't. Frantically, she tugged a loaded vegetable rack to hold it while she searched for an escape.

There was a door to the outside across the room. That would have been a gift from heaven but for the fact that it simply opened on to a plot of earth where Zina did the washing, and was surrounded by an unscalable thorny hedge.

Desperate as she was, however, she ran out there and looked for a place to hide. Anything was better than calmly giving herself up to Nick in his present mood.

Her heart pounding in her throat, she crouched behind a washtub among other laundry items at the side of the door.

She heard Nick make short work of the loaded vegetable rack. He strode out and cast a brief glance around, then moved towards the hedge as though he half suspected that she might have attempted to evade him in that direction.

His hesitation was long enough for her to lurch back inside the door. Skidding over scattered vegetables, she reached the hall before her ruse had time to register on him.

She knew she would never make it across the living-room to the outdoors so, desperate again, she fled to her room, then hardly able to control her shaking hands as he followed in hot pursuit she turned the key in the lock.

White-faced, she heard his heavy breathing outside and his incensed tones. 'Don't play hide and seek with me, Lindsey. It won't get you anywhere.'

He began to put pressure on the door. His shoulder crashed against it again and again, and she watched horrified as the lock began to give under the force. Wildly she glanced around the room, realising her folly in shutting herself off in this way. But who would have thought he would be so crazed as to break down the door?

The window sills were too high to get a purchase without a chair or something. She turned her terrified gaze back to the splintering lock and decided it was her only hope.

The door burst open before she was half-way across the room. Nick, a lock of dark hair over his brow making him look infinitely more menacing, strolled in.

She steadied herself beside the bed, on the point of collapse now. She had used up the last vestiges of her strength in trying to elude him. Fear and panic had made havoc of her nervous system so that she was drained of all but a deep revulsion for the man who approached her.

'You should find that ring I gave you, Lindsey.' Though his face was flushed with rage, his smile was playful. 'When I put it on your finger it was to claim you as mine.' She tensed with distaste as he smoothed a strand of hair on her shoulder. 'And what Nick Mollenda puts a claim on, he keeps.'

It flashed into Lindsey's mind that this was a different Nick to the one who had been cringing at the thought of going against his parents' wishes at the mansion. But she knew better than to rile him further by mentioning it. She knew also that he didn't see her as flesh and blood so much as a stepping stone to the bauxite wealth he craved.

He put a finger under her chin and tilted it so that she was compelled to meet his gaze. Her hands were clenched at her sides, not with staunchness, for she was too limp for that, but with abject loathing at his touch.

And this was the man she had been rushing headlong into marriage with! She must have been insane to think she could spend one night, let alone a lifetime, in his arms.

She forced some resonance into her voice, though it

came out lamentably faint as she said, 'You're going to be in a great deal more trouble than you are now when my father returns and learns how you've been conducting yourself in his house. You can hardly make it appear that I turned to you for ... affection,' she could barely mouth the word, 'with the signs of violence around here.'

If she had hoped to distract him by highlighting the fact that he was losing sight of his original purpose, she was disappointed.

'For one thing,' the finger traced her jawline, 'we won't be here. As I said at the start, you and I are going to make a little trip.' While her strangled heart recovered slightly at the ray of hope his words had sparked in her, he went on, 'For another, I don't particularly care how I achieve my aims as long as I get what I want in the end.'

Before she had a chance to make any sense out of this last portion of his reply, his caressing hand turned into a cruel vice on her arm. 'No more games, darling. At least not for the time being.' He spared her a succinct gleam. 'We're going out to my car and I don't need to warn you that my patience is becoming a little threadbare at your persistence in evading your betrothal promises.'

If he had but known it, Lindsey needed no encouragement, either forced or otherwise, to escape the unbearable intimacy of her bedroom. Though if she had had any inkling as to what lay ahead she wouldn't have been so eager to leave.

# CHAPTER TEN

ONCE outside, the storm-charged air did little to help her shattered nerves. And sealed in beside Nick in the shooting brake, she began to feel infinitely more helpless than she had done in the house. *Where was he taking her? What lunacy was he embarking on now in the frantic hope of solving his financial worries?*

She resolved to stay silent, but after some moments out on the road when he turned in the direction of the forests, she blurted, 'Nick, this is madness. You know what the rain's like at this time of year. We could be washed away. You're as familiar with the signs as I am. In a short while we're going to be caught in a deluge that will make driving impossible.'

'That's what I'm hoping,' he nodded, unperturbed. 'Though I think you're a little precipitous with your forecast. As you say, I'm familiar with the signs and to my way of reckoning we have ample time to reach our destination before the storm breaks.'

Unfortunately, though it had been worth a try, she knew that he was right. The sulphurous skies would nurse their contents, as was the way in Guyana, until the last drop of water forced the tide of clouds to open up in a downward torrent.

Her throat tight and painful, Lindsey racked her brain for some way out of her predicament. The thought of leaving a speeding car was ludicrous. And what other possibilities were there? No, her lips trembled, she was trapped alone with Nick for the moment. All she could do was wait and grasp an opportunity to escape him later—if one arose.

As they ploughed deeper and deeper into the forest, this small ray of hope grew more dim with every mile. How could she possibly expect to run from him out here in the wilds? And who could she turn to for help should she be lucky enough to elude him for a few brief moments?

In her frantic state it was some time before the familiarity of the route dawned on her. And as it slowly did so, a new fear gripped her. She may have viewed these monkey- and bird-populated stretches with affectionate regard in the past, but now they instilled in her a particular kind of dread.

'Nick,' she burst out, 'where are you taking me? Why don't you stop this nonsense and turn round and go home? If you turn back now, I promise I won't say a word about this to my father.'

When she saw that he intended to ignore her pleas she asked sharply, 'Just where are you planning on going? There's nowhere in this direction where we'll be safe from the downpour when it comes.'

'There's one place.' He looked at her. 'I'm surprised you haven't guessed before now.' Knowing that she had, he elaborated, 'The last place anyone will think of looking for us is Mackenzie's vacated log cabin. Out in the middle of nowhere it's perfect for a ... loving couple like us, and I wouldn't be likely to agree to making our pre-nuptial nest in the very spot where my fiancée was, er ... compromised by a rival.'

Brance! Brance! Her heart cried out for him now. Why hadn't she listened to him when he had tried to warn her against Nick?

'Whatever you're hoping to achieve by this monstrous behaviour,' she was reduced to saying in choked tones, 'you'll never succeed. My father will be more likely to have you thrown in jail rather than agree to your demands when he finds out about your callous conduct.'

'You're wrong, Lindsey,' he shot her a merciless smile. 'I'm bound to succeed. You haven't heard the other half of my plan yet.'

Lindsey slumped in her seat. It was obvious she was not going to be able to reason with Nick. His mind unbalanced by the build-up of pressure concerning his debts, he had arrived at the state where he would try anything to avoid ruin. And she couldn't imagine what he meant by 'the other half of his plan'. Surely what he had schemed thus far was the apex in villainy.

Since she had discovered that they were making for Brance's disused log cabin another tiny spark of hope had glimmered through her growing anxiety. This died when they drove past Danny Capucho's store and she saw that it was all barred and shuttered.

Of course! There would be no business for the Indian trader now that the rainy season had truly set in. He usually spent this period lining up produce in Georgetown.

Sinking lower in her seat, she stifled the tears of frustration that threatened.

When they arrived at the spot where the cabin was situated she clung to a last, small hope that the log structure would be equally barred and shuttered. But there were no precious possessions of Brance's there now; no expensive forestry equipment which must be locked away against inquisitive Indians straying from the store.

Coming upon the cabin in the gloom, she saw with sinking heart that it had been left much as most vacated premises are left, neat and tidy and open for inspection. Though the door was closed against marauding animals and destructive monkeys, it opened at a touch of the catch as Nick seemed to know it would do. His hand gripping her arm, for he had made sure as soon as they left the car that she should not stray from him, he thrust her before him now.

Entering the cabin, filled with memories for so short a stay, was like a blow to Lindsey. Never had she felt so bereft of Brance as she did now. The nostalgia of his going was unendurable here, where he had spent so many weeks living and working in the forests. Every item in the room seemed imbued with his vibrant personality, so that it was all she could do not to drop down on the bed and open the floodgates of her heartache.

She was brought back to the ugly present by Nick's touch. Turning an arm about her waist, he murmured, 'Looks like we're going to be very comfortable here, darling. Mackenzie has very kindly left all his trappings, no doubt for Ben's use while he supervises his plant-gathering. It would surprise the forestry man to know that you and I have found it a most convenient spot in which to be together.'

He began to trail his fingers through her hair. A sob in her throat, Lindsey strove to speak calmly. 'Nick, I beg you to see sense. All this is going to get you nowhere . . .'

Mercilessly he cupped her chin in his fingers and brought his mouth down on her lips. But there was no passion there, nothing; a fact that she was thankful for, though she struggled in revulsion at his kiss.

He raised his head, his dark eyes sparking at her distaste. His smile held cruel amusement. 'Considering that you once agreed to become my wife, you're not very accommodating to my needs, my sweet,' he complained.

He seemed to enjoy her repulsion and finding ways of increasing it; like lowering a caressing hand towards the top button of her blouse. Yet she was struck by the absence of lust in his manner, the cold way he made his advances. Somehow his kind of lovemaking was far more sinister than that of a full-blooded male, craving satisfaction.

She set her teeth as he lowered his head and caressed the hollow of her breasts with his lips. She had time to glance round wildly for something to take up in her hand as a weapon. She was fixing her gaze on an iron implement nearby, when he abruptly raised his head and released her from his brutal grip.

He seemed to derive more amusement from the startled, wondering expression on her face.

'I'm going to forgo your irresistible womanly charms for the moment, my dear Lindsey,' he told her. His merciless smile lapsing disdainfully he went on, 'I've no wish to saddle myself with a wife and a brat ... unless of course I'm given no other choice. That will depend entirely on your father.'

Lindsey was so overcome with relief at being free of his hold on her, she tottered to a safer distance without paying a lot of attention to his words. But she gathered hazily that this must be the rest of the plan he had spoken of.

'I shall leave a note at Springlands,' he was saying. 'It will inform him that he will never see his daughter again unless he agrees to sell me the land as we originally arranged.'

If Lindsey hadn't been so sure that he was in deadly earnest in all he said, she would have laughed out loud at his melodramatic imagination. But because she knew Nick had every intention of achieving his aims no matter how bizarre his methods, she was bound to ask coldly, 'And if he refuses?'

'Then you and I will disappear for a while to my property in Brazil. Oh yes, we'll turn up one day,' he hurried to assure her, his dark gleam meaningful, '. . . the three of us. And, past quarrels forgotten by then, Ben will be ready, I'm sure, to receive his ... family.'

Though his reasoning was not that of a sound mind, there was potentially a possibility of success in what he proposed.

'I'm sure you'll be wasting your time with that kind of condition.' Her querulous tones lacked conviction. 'My father will not be intimidated by your demands.'

'We shall see,' Nick said confidently. 'He will have twenty-four hours to make up his mind. After which, if I have received no satisfaction, I shall be back, my dear, to ... take up where we left off ...'

The knowledge that he planned to leave her, to go all the way back to Springlands, far, far away from her was like a chorus of heavenly voices in her ears. Afraid now to say anything that might make him change his mind in this direction, she hovered, desisting from wringing her hands as he strolled around.

'It looks as though you'll be comfortable while I'm away,' he said. 'There's everything to make your stay pleasant, even including a small stock of food still on the shelf. How thoughtful of Mackenzie, don't you think, to provide for our possible stay here in this way?'

All Lindsey was waiting for was the moment when he drove away. She held her breath and prayed that he wouldn't have a quixotic change of mind at the last minute. But Nick appeared to be very lucid in his arrangement of things—right down to reading her mind on one particular point.

Inclining his head to indicate the thunder which had been rattling around the skies for some time, and glancing towards the almost non-existent light through the windows, he mentioned leisurely, 'In case you're entertaining any ideas of leaving here on foot once I've gone, I should think twice about it, if I were you. There's no help within miles of this place and the only road out of here is likely to be awash for a while. I should hate to think of you drowning in a torrent while I'm doing all I can to secure your continued well-being.'

As though aware then of his own impending predicament in the approaching storm, he strode swiftly to the door. 'You'll excuse me if I hurry now, my sweet. I have a long drive ahead of me. But don't feel lonely.' His ruthless mouth curved into the semblance of a smile. 'If things don't go according to my wishes, I'll be back to, er . . . take up where we left off.'

Lindsey felt a colossal weight fall from her when he stepped outside. Though she was tempted to rush forward and slam the door behind him, she resisted the urge. A padlock, even if she knew where it was, was no use to her on an outside clasp. Also she felt it prudent to be cautious until he was actually on his way.

That blissful moment came a short while later. Without a backward glance either in mock concern or cruel amusement, he took the powerful shooting brake forward, the noise of its engine lost in that of the rumbling heavens. Seconds later the vehicle was disappearing through the trees, noiselessly and phantom-like in the leaden light.

Crumpling then, Lindsey reeled towards the bed and fell face downward there. But burying her face in the pillow did not shut out the lurid scenes that tormented her mind. Nick had gone now, but he would be back. He would return as he had said he would. There was one reason why she was blood-chillingly certain of this.

He had said he would leave a note at Springlands and wait only twenty-four hours at the sugar estate for some message from Ben. But her father wouldn't be home in twenty-four hours.

Nick thought that Ben and Sam had gone on an overnight fishing trip. He didn't know that they planned to do some work at the saw-mill and didn't intend to return to Springlands until Monday morning!

Lindsey had known, but she had said nothing of the men's prolonged stay away from the house to Nick. She had almost ruined her father once. She didn't intend to be the willing instrument of bringing possible disaster to him a second time.

Her skin crawled when she thought of Nick's return. She had heard that gamblers in life derived their thrills from the excitement of winning; that would explain his stony approach as a lover. But she knew he would go ahead with his plan to father a Davis child in the hope of appealing to Ben's staunch family beliefs.

The rain started in loud spattering drops on the leaves beyond the doorway. Soon they were making a drumming, plashing sound as trees and jungle greenery came under the tremendous force of swollen clouds releasing their contents.

Lindsey rose and hurried to close the cabin door, a new fear gripping her. *Supposing Nick didn't make it on the dirt road out of the forests? Supposing he got cut off in the downpour and had to turn back!*

She prayed that the rain wouldn't hamper his progress. For the best part of an hour she sat on the bed, hands clenched on her lap, flinching at every sound that might be that of his car returning. Only when she was certain that he had truly gone until tomorrow at this time, did she feel safe enough to fall back limply on the bed.

When she had regained a little of her strength she lit the lamp to combat the darkness of night, and took stock of her situation. There wasn't a moment to lose. She must think of something that would remove her from Nick's threats when he returned.

At first light she could try and make it to the nearest

Indian village. It was an optimistic thought, but her heart sank when she considered the possibility. She was not equipped to travel across country. Even if the rain had ceased by morning, she knew none of the paths through savannah and forest which the Indians used by habit. She could end up lost before she had gone half a mile.

Another choice was to hide somewhere among the trees at the hour of Nick's return—but he would find her. He was obsessed with his scheme which he believed would put him in line for the bauxite wealth. He wouldn't let a few square yards of greenery come between him and his goal.

Though all her feminine instincts urged her to put as much distance as she could between herself and the cabin before his return, she knew that her only sure defence was the cabin itself. True, she had no means of bolting and barring the door, but she could barricade herself in. There were lots of items in the room; the trestle table, the stove—anything she could lay her hands on. The log cabin was a sturdy structure, built by her father's men. Nick would have a hard time forcing his way in when she had finished. And if she could only gain time by keeping him at bay, it would be better than offering no resistance at all.

Having decided on her plan of action she slid between the sheets and tried to get some rest. Tomorrow was going to be a gruelling day. She would need all the strength she could muster to get through it.

During the night, the storm lashed the forest. The rain thundered down on the roof and in between fitful snatches of sleep, Lindsey was warmed by the thought that perhaps she would be marooned here for several days. Perhaps, with roads awash, Nick would not be able to make the trip back here as he had threatened!

But perverse as fate often is, by morning, the storm had moved on. Still she clung to the faint hope that the deluge might have been catastrophic enough further afield to hinder his return.

Certainly there were floods everywhere outside the cabin. And it was not unknown for dirt roads to cave in under pressure of water.

This was a heartening thought, but not one she dare trust in completely. After some strong coffee and a meal of sorts to bolster her energy, she set about piling things behind the door.

By the end of the afternoon she doubted if half a dozen men would have the joint force to gain entry. The trestle table was of heavy hardwood. It had taken her half the morning to drag it across the room and prop it up horizontally in position. To prevent it from sliding with pressure she had hammered, with her shoe, several chips of kindling wood to wedge it at the point where it rested on the floor. This, combined with everything else she could find stowed against it, made, if she said it herself, an effective deterrent for anyone to try and enter.

A glance at her watch set her heart thumping. The twenty-four hours were almost up. She cast a quick look around and realised with flying nerves that she had given no thought to the window!

Luckily there were shutters that she could pull to and latch on the inside, and the window itself had a sturdy fastener. Any more than this, she had neither the time nor the implements for improvements.

She could have done with a cup of coffee to steady her shaking limbs, but she had let the stove go out. She had this vague notion that if she guarded against displaying any signs of her presence inside, Nick might quickly grow tired of hammering on the door and go away.

It was cold and damp waiting for his arrival. The bed had gone along with everything else to join the heap behind the door. All she had to sit on was a rough wooden container used to store dry firewood.

The minutes dragged by, became half an hour, an hour, two hours. The light faded. Though Lindsey was sat in considerable gloom with door and shutters closed, there were enough chinks between the logs and window to know that night was setting in.

She rose from her cramped position and began to pace. Even allowing for the outward journey before the twenty-four hours came into force, Nick had had ample time now to make the return trip.

She felt a slight lifting of her spirits. Was it as she had hoped? Had he been cut off somewhere, prevented by a flooded river, perhaps, from making it back to the cabin? She dared not set too much store by this conjecture, but certainly as time dragged on it seemed that it might possibly be correct.

She waited poised until the early hours, then finally relaxed. All her efforts to shut herself in now seemed faintly ridiculous. Well, at least it had helped to pass the time, she mused wryly. Tomorrow she would set about making herself more comfortable here, as she was apparently marooned for some time.

She was thinking of dragging the bed to a spot where she could try and get warm enough between the blankets to sleep awhile when a blood-chilling sound came to her ears on the forest silence. It was that of an engine—a car engine—and it was drawing rapidly closer.

Her heart catapulting into her throat, she stumbled to peep through a crack in the logs. Her line of vision showed only the dripping open space fronting the cabin. But even as she watched the patch was being illuminated by the powerful beam of car headlights.

She waited then, mouth dry, her legs almost buckling beneath her as she saw the shooting brake slew to a stop. *Nick was back!* He had been delayed and, by the sound of his driving, he was in an ugly mood.

Trembling violently, she crept back to her seat. She heart the slam of the car door, the purposeful footsteps splashing up to the cabin.

The next ten minutes were the worst she had ever lived through. All ways were tried to gain entry into the cabin. She could hear him battering at the door, trying the shutters.

After a while there was a period of complete silence. She inclined her head listening for any extraneous noises, but the loud roaring of blood in her ears muffled her hearing. When she could steady herself sufficiently to come to grips with what was going on outside, it was to realise with an insidious horror that the shutters were being forced.

The window! She had been known in her heart that this was the most vulnerable of her defences. Even as she stared, the shutters were beginning to give under pressure. It was only a question of minutes before the clasp fell apart. Then a man as desperate as Nick, had only to break the glass, find the window catch with his hand and vault inside.

Suddenly an unmitigated anger rose in her. The thought that she had gone to all that effort to be beaten by an unbarricadeable window, set her bosom heaving with an out and out determination to retaliate. She certainly was not going to sit here and calmly accept Nick's ultimatum.

Reaching down into the fuel box beneath her, her fingers closed round a stout club of timber. She had the advantage of being able to crouch in wait for him when he came through the window. And she would have no compunction—no sir!—in bringing her club down squarely on his skull before he had time to set more than a foot in the room.

Though every part of her was shaking as she crept to take up her position, it was mainly Davis temper which motivated her actions. She might have been sick with fright yesterday when Nick had taken her by surprise, but she had had time to prepare herself now, as he was about to discover at any moment.

She heard the shutters being ripped back off their hinges. The window was a mere formality to a man in his frame of mind.

The glass splintered. She caught a faint reflection of the car headlights in the shards that fell to the floor, then she heard the catch of the window being clawed at; the window being thrown apart.

She was ready. More than ready. How dared he subject her to this kind of nerve-racking experience? He would be lucky if she didn't brain him after all he had put her through!

She raised her arm, poised for action. She saw the dark figure land inside the room, and then she aimed. In the split second before her club found its mark the figure, as though sensing a presence, whipped round. A dark oath rent the gloom while a flash of thought travelled across her consciousness, that there was something oddly different about Nick's shape.

It was enough to make her club hand falter; though it would never have reached its target, for she was grabbed in the same split-second. She was about to give Nick a thorny reception when something about that nearness doused the fight in her.

That masterful hold . . . those uncompromising arms . . . that familiar denim-shirted chest. It was then that her knees gave way as Brance bit out urgently in the darkness, 'Lindsey! Are you okay?'

On a laugh that was half sob she replied, 'Yes . . . I'm okay.' But to her befuddled mind nothing made sense.

In the scant glow from the headlights, she wanted to feast her eyes on Brance's face. It was not the old Brance she knew. His features were weary, tortured and grim.

He strained her close to him, his hands exploring every inch of her as though he expected to find her in pieces in some way. He came upon the stout rod of wood in her hand and a grin of sorts split his brooding expression. 'That's my Lindsey! Never one to go down without putting up a ruckus,' he growled. 'Well, I don't intend to go through another day like yesterday. And I reckon it's time I harnessed that logging woman cussedness before it gets us into any more sticky situations. We're getting married first thing in the morning. You hear?'

'Yes, Brance,' she said meekly, a rosy mist filling her mind.

'I've lived an indescribable hell since last night, wondering what had happened to you. But I don't plan to let you put me on that kind of rack again. As my wife you'll listen to reason. Right?'

'Right,' she said, his anger like music in her ears.

He kissed her then, long and tenderly, his wrath a mere safety valve for his exploding relief.

His fingers gently released the club from her hand and as it dropped to the floor, she said in mild panic at what she might have done, 'I saw the shooting brake. I thought it was Nick—why didn't you let me know you were outside?'

'I called your name a couple of times,' his voice shook imperceptibly. 'But then I couldn't let myself . . .'

'You didn't think that I . . .?'

'Mollenda is capable of anything,' he gripped her close. 'But if he had harmed a hair of your head, I would have strung him up personally.'

Basking in the safety of his arms, she said trance-like, 'Brance ... I don't understand. What are you doing here? I thought you would have been in Perú by now.'

'It's a long story,' he gave her a jaded smile. 'And one you're in no condition to hear at the moment. You can hardly stand, and your skin's like ice. Where's the lamp?'

Purposefully he arranged some illumination, spread a blanket on the floor, with the wall as a backrest and led her to sink down there.

'There's no time to do a lot here,' he said, stowing wood in the stove. 'Georgetown is flooded and the fresh bout of rain is headed this way. This area's likely to be cut off for weeks, so a couple of hours is our limit.'

In a fraction of that time he had coffee made and a hot meal. The stove spread a comforting warmth through the haphazard interior. The beef stew was like ambrosia on Lindsey's tongue. Brance didn't eat, though he lounged at the side of her, watching the colour steal back into her cheeks.

With every mouthful, she cast him an impatient smile. In the end, one long leg drawn up to support his coffee-mug hand, he relented and launched into the explanation she couldn't wait to hear.

'The thing that put Mollenda's scheme out of joint,' he began 'was an uneasiness on Ben's part concerning you. After I left, he and Sam went fishing, right? They planned to stay away the weekend. The two old guys were peeved over something, it seemed ...' With an answering smile to Lindsey's gleam which seemed to say, can't you guess what? he went on, 'By evening they got to feeling a little ashamed of their behaviour. They'd have been okay in the saw-mill, but they reckoned it wasn't right to leave you alone in the house with a storm brewing, so they packed up and came home.'

'Your Dad found Mollenda's note. He was almost out of his mind when he saw your splintered door and chaos in the kitchen. It was Sam who kept him from going off his head, and came up with the idea that they ought to try and contact yours truly for advice. He drove Ben to Moratica. There they tried to get in touch with me, by phone, in Georgetown, but I wasn't in Georgetown.'

'You weren't?' Lindsey blinked.

He shook his head. 'I'd left the hotel and was on my way back to Springlands. By the time I arrived, some time after midnight, Ben and Sam were all for crashing in on Mollenda at the mansion. But having heard the story—and seen the evidence,' he added grimly, 'I reckoned we should bluff out the stipulated twenty-four hours, after which I would be lying in wait for Mollenda when he started out, supposedly on his way back to you.'

'Unfortunately he got wind of my trailing him and ducked off in another direction. It was quite a chase. I hung on to him almost as far as Caibo, where I cornered him at a flooded junction of the river. Hauling him from his seat took no effort at all, the way I felt. Once I'd . . . er . . . coaxed out of him where he had you tucked away, I gave him a choice. He could either disappear, or I'd cart him back to the mansion to explain a few discrepancies in the sugar-cane profits.

'Needless to say, as that's only the tip of the iceberg, concerning his debts, he opted for spending the next decade or so in some spot he's got in Brazil.'

'But how come you arrived here in his shooting brake?' Lindsey asked as he refilled her coffee mug.

'I reckoned it was better for shipping water in these parts, and I had to think of bringing you back with more rain threatening. I left Mollenda to make his own way, but I was plagued with the thought, as I drove here, that he might decide to cut across country and try and reach you first. He knows these parts better than I do. I had visions of arriving here and . . .'

Lindsey lowered her mug and snuggled up to rest her head on his shoulder. She could see now why he had made his entry through the window so uncertainly.

'I wonder what the old Mollendas will do without Nick?' she asked staring at the glow in the stove.

'It's Steve Albengo, the overseer, who does all the work. Apparently he's had his suspicions for some time that the sugar-cane turnover is not what it should be. One of the sons-in-law—a wizard at business security, by all accounts—is due to arrive any time now to look into the figures. That's what pressured Nick into trying to push that bauxite deal through, so that he could replace the missing sugar-estate funds from mining company advances, before they were discovered.'

'I thought there must be something to make him act so wildly,' Lindsey said slowly. 'Nick is usually so cool about everything.'

'He was cool, all right,' Brance said drily, seeing it in another sense.

There was a silence, but only a brief one, for Lindsey was still eager to know the reason for a particular glow in her heart.

'Brance,' she said carefully, 'you drove to Georgetown when you left us at Springlands, right?'

'Right,' he nodded.

'And you booked in for an overnight stay at your usual hotel there, right?'

'Right,' he grinned as though he knew what was coming.

'Then why,' she turned to fiddle with the collar of his denim jacket so that she could see the look in his eyes, 'did you decide to drive back to Springlands?'

She was well rewarded by the light she saw in his gaze. He kissed her slowly to tease her a little, then he explained, 'I didn't make immediately for Georgetown when I'd said goodbye to you all. I stopped off in Moratica first to settle my dues there. I had one or two bills to clear up. When I got to Georgetown I spent a pretty depressing session in my room. Despite our abrasive tangles at every meeting, I'd always been fairly certain that, beneath the sparks, you felt something deep and lasting for me. But that parting peck on the cheek threw me. I figured I must have been wrong about your feelings where I was concerned.

'I drove away wanting to burn up the road as I felt I was burning up inside with my need for you. To give myself something to do in my room, to take my mind off you, I took to flicking through the bills I'd paid in Moratica. There was one for Nancy's stay at the hotel, and in the same envelope I found a slip listing the cost of a hired car to Springlands. I knew then that Nancy had been to see you. And I reckoned I could make a pretty good guess why you had given me that peck on the cheek.'

'I saw you with her in Georgetown,' Lindsey revealed, not quite meeting his gaze. 'You seemed intent on making her stay agreeable.'

'She'd come a long way to see me,' he shrugged. 'Every two or three years she took it into her head to visit me on the job. We'd have a pleasant time together, but she could never wait to get back to Sackville.'

'Is that why she came to Moratica?' Lindsey asked. 'To see you in your work surroundings?'

'More or less. I'd planned to show her the log cabin

here, but with the scandal at its height she displayed a kind of frozen reluctance to have anything to do with the idea.' There was a steely twinkle in his eye.

'You've known Nancy a long time,' she fiddled with his shirt button.

'We were childhood sweethearts,' he nodded, his lips lowered to her fingers. 'But we're two mature people now. I think Nancy recognises that.' And drawing her close, 'You're the woman I want to spend the rest of my life with. I've loved you since the first day I saw you, preparing to drown yourself on that matchwood raft.'

'I wasn't planning any such thing! And that matchwood raft——'

'End of argument—at least on that score,' he said, closing off her protests with his lips.

A long moment later she stretched luxuriously in his arms. 'Mmmm! It's so cosy here. How long did you say we were going to be marooned in these parts?'

Catching her meaning, he pushed her gently away. 'Don't tempt me. Besides, one last remaining can of stew is not sufficient nourishment to sustain a guy on his honeymoon.' With a wicked gleam he rose and pulled her to her feet.

To give them both something useful to do he added, 'You douse the stove down, and I'll clear this mess away from the door. Your Dad and Sam will be hanging on, waiting for news of you.'

The warm flush of romance receding fractionally in the light of more pressing practicalities, Lindsey did as he said.

'I'm looking forward to seeing their faces when they know they've finally got you for a son-in-law,' she commented drily.

'We'll make their day and have a splash wedding at the Moratica hotel,' Brance told her. 'Then we'll have to catch that plane for Peru.'

Once outside, with the door closed behind them, he picked her up in his arms for the muddy trek to the car. 'Reckon you're going to take to being a forestry man's wife?' he asked, nuzzling his chin in her hair.

'Try me,' she said '. . . for about the next forty years.' And clasping her arms about his neck, 'I love you, Brance. Have done since the day you ruined my trip downriver on that superstructure raft of mine——'

'Superstructure! Why, that——'

'End of argument,' she said sweetly, nuzzling his ear.

He grinned, kissed her, and dumped her into her seat. 'There's one thing I'll say,' he said, climbing in behind the wheel. 'The next forty years promise to be anything but dull with you tagging along on my travels.'

'Anything *but*,' she murmured, sloping him a look while she crowded him in his seat.

'Give a guy room to drive, will you,' he complained with a glint. 'One of us has to get this thing back to civilisation. Furthermore, I still have to make an honest woman of you, remember?'

'Yes, Brance,' she settled down, meekly but twinklingly, in her seat.

The drive back to Springlands promised to be a rough one; just as life alongside Brance in his work might be at times. She was not deterred. Love could surmount the most formidable obstacles.

With their over-abundance of it, there was nothing they couldn't do together.

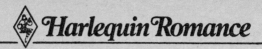
**Harlequin Romance**

## Coming Next Month

**2839   ODD MAN OUT  Sharron Cohen**
A chauffeur's daughter's hand in marriage is priceless—both to her fiancé and to his estranged brother, her first great love. Would he use that love just to give his rival a run for his money?

**2840   FOR KARIN'S SAKE  Samantha Day**
A young widow is just beginning to feel whole again when her heart goes out to a troubled child and her uncompromising father. But is he suggesting marriage—just for the sake of his daughter?

**2841   THE MARATI LEGACY  Dana James**
Although she's still haunted by the pain of a past experience, an oceanographer joins a search for sunken treasure off the Madagascar coast. She finds adventure, but she also finds love—and is frightened by its intensity.

**2842   IMMUNE TO LOVE  Claudia Jameson**
No one is immune to love. But when a career girl falls for her charming boss, she's afraid she'll contract permanent heartache. Unless she can discover why he suddenly pulls away from her...

**2843   RING OF CLADDAGH  Annabel Murray**
Claddagh Hall is left jointly to a London fashion designer and the rightful heir, a provocative and teasing Irishman. But it's no joking matter when he proposes marriage!

**2844   MOROCCAN MADNESS  Angela Wells**
After their whirlwind courtship, her Moroccan husband accused her of betraying him on their wedding night. Now he wants her back. To continue the madness that drove her away? Or to rekindle the love that still smolders between them?

Available in June wherever paperback books are sold, or through Harlequin Reader Service.

In the U.S.
901 Fuhrmann Blvd.
P.O. Box 1397
Buffalo, N.Y.  14240-1397

In Canada
P.O. Box 603
Fort Erie, Ontario
L2A 5X3

# What the press says about Harlequin romance fiction...

"When it comes to romantic novels...
Harlequin is the indisputable king."
— *New York Times*

"...always with an upbeat, happy ending."
— *San Francisco Chronicle*

"Women have come to trust these
stories about contemporary people,
set in exciting foreign places."
— *Best Sellers*, New York

"The most popular reading matter of
American women today."
— *Detroit News*

"...a work of art."
— *Globe & Mail*, Toronto

# Can you keep a secret?

## You can keep this one plus 4 free novels

## Janet Dailey

### Americana

A romantic tour of America with
Janet Dailey!

Enjoy two releases each month from this
collection of your favorite previously
published Janet Dailey titles, presented
alphabetically state by state.

Available NOW wherever paperback books
are sold.

**For the millions who can't read
Give the Gift of Literacy**

One out of five adults in North America
cannot read or write well enough
to fill out a job application
or understand the directions on a bottle of medicine.

**You can change all this by joining the fight
against illiteracy.**

For more information write to:
Contact, Box 81826, Lincoln, Neb.  68501
In the United States, call toll free: 800-228-3225

**The only degree you need
is a degree of caring**